GOLD

&

GREED

GOLD
&
GREED

Murdoch in Muskoka
Book II

Liam D. Dwyer

MUSKOKA DOCKSIDE READER

Published by Muskoka Dockside Reader
Box 444, Bracebridge, Ontario P1L 1T7

Library and Archives Canada Cataloguing in Publication

Dwyer, Liam D., 1923-
Gold & Greed : Murdoch in Muskoka, book II / Liam D. Dwyer.

Sequel to : Murder in Muskoka.
ISBN 0-9736208-1-1

1. Muskoka (Ont. : District municipality) — Fiction. I. Title.

PS8607.W94G74 2005   C813.6   C2005-905015-2

This book is a work of fiction.
Any resemblance of characters in the story to individuals,
living or dead, is purely coincidental.

Cover photograph
Lake Muskoka sunset, by Brad Hammond

Design and typesetting by Fox Meadow Creations
www.foxmeadowbooks.com
Printed and bound in Canada by Métrolitho
Text typeface is Minion
PERMANENT PAPER ∞

Dedicated to Debera, Janna and Lori

PROLOGUE

FINALLY, AFTER FIVE LONG YEARS, opportunity had dropped in his lap. God, how he hated his job, sucking up to rich bastards just to eat and pay the rent. You couldn't rent a cheap one-room apartment in Boca Raton, Florida, constantly dealing with multi-millionaires, and not feel some resentment.

But for Peter Crawford, that was all about to change.

Mr. Jose de Sa, one of the rich bastards, came into the bank on the second Tuesday of every month. He followed an exact routine. He signed the appointment book with an illegible scrawl, and it was only after someone deciphered the broken hieroglyphics that they knew all he wanted was to visit his safe deposit boxes. He had two of the largest, each ten by ten inches.

On alternate Tuesdays he would sign the Safe Deposit Box Ledger and his signature would be verified. Then he'd present his two keys. An attendant would insert the bank's key in one lock while de Sa would insert his in the other. The door would be opened and both steel boxes slid out. They were heavy, and the owner needed assistance carrying them to a private cubical. When the two boxes were safely in Mr. de Sa's possession he'd lock the door against prying eyes. Each time, after at least a half hour, he'd ask for assistance to return them to their proper location in the vault. Peter had noticed a slight tremor in de Sa's right hand, possibly the beginning of Parkinson's disease.

On one of these Tuesdays a bank clerk, a petite woman, was unable to lift down the heavy box and called Peter to help. After Peter had put them in de Sa's cubical he went back to his desk. From that day on, every idle moment was spent wondering what was in those boxes—and if it was worth the effort to steal. A plan began to hatch in Peter Crawford's mind.

It wasn't going to be easy determining the contents of the boxes. For the next Tuesday visit, Peter made sure he was on the floor at the exact time Jose de Sa arrived. At the conclusion of his usual half hour, when the old man asked for assistance, Peter carried the first of the boxes back to the vault. Returning for the second, he noticed a coin had fallen to the carpeted floor of the cubical. What a stroke of luck! He pushed it under the table with his foot and took the second box to the vault where the old man saw that both were safely in place. As was de Sa's habit, he quickly left the bank.

Back in the cubical, Peter picked the coin from the floor. It was in a small plastic envelope. He examined it very carefully. Although he'd never seen a gold coin before, he was sure it was gold. The coin was heavy, perhaps an ounce, the face of a woman with stars surrounding her head on one side. On her crown was one word, LIBERTY, and at the bottom was the year, 1907. Turning the coin, Peter saw the crest of the United States of America. The denomination engraved at the bottom was a surprise. Twenty dollars. He examined it again, memorizing its weight and image. Then he quickly ran to the parking lot where he was just able to stop de Sa from leaving. When the old man opened the window of his Bentley, Peter showed him the coin.

The old man's jaw dropped. He looked at the coin in Peter's hand in disbelief before snatching it up and thrusting it into his jacket pocket. De Sa started to drive away, then stopped the car with a jerk and backed up, almost hitting a dumbfounded Peter. In broken English, de Sa apologized profusely. He produced a thick roll of hundred-dollar bills and peeled off two, which he tried to stuff into Peter's jacket pocket.

"Oh, I can't take that money. It's company policy, Mr. de Sa. I was just doing my job."

A couple hundred bucks reward for finding one coin? Peter Crawford realized he was on to something big. He'd now use this friendship to further his scheme.

The next step was to determine the value of the coin and estimate the quantity in each of the boxes. For this exercise, he assumed they were all the same as the one he'd held in his hand. Once at home, he Googled for "gold coins minted 1907." The search immediately located colour photos of an identical coin, both head and tail, selling at that moment for $1,856.00. According to the numismatic website, it had a weight of 0.96750 ounces of pure gold. In May of 1989, it had sold for $4,525.00.

"Son of a bitch," Peter whispered.

Over the next few weeks, Peter ascertained the empty weight of a safe deposit box, then subtracted that from the approximate weight of each of de Sa's full ones. For a ballpark calculation, he used two thousand dollars for each coin, hoping that de Sa wouldn't have misplaced his most expensive possession. If both boxes were filled with coins, there could be as much as $800,000 in each box. Old man de Sa probably had $1,600,000 stashed away. Peter would have to knock off some weight for the plastic covers around the coins, of course. He settled on an even million as the value of both boxes. A conservative estimate for sure.

Jose de Sa lived in Royal Palm, a gated community of Boca Raton. The area had its own security, with two cruisers parked at the Federal Highway entrance. Peter nonchalantly drove through the Camino Real entrance, passing a security officer with a wave of his hand. The homes were enormous, with two or three garages each. The series of canals connecting to the Inter-Coastal Waterway appeared littered with yacht or sailboat masts visible between the houses.

Peter finally found de Sa's address. It was an enormous villa with curved driveway, three-car garage and a portico that could park three more vehicles. The front door was entirely glass, rising all the way to a second floor where it met a curved balcony over the portico. A massive chandelier was visible from the street.

Peter knew enough not to linger. There would be cameras recording every move inside the gated community, and someone would be monitoring every movement. He'd seen enough, but just who was Jose de Sa?

The people who know most about any residential compound like Royal Palm are the people who serve them—the little guys like Peter himself. Golf pros, caddies, groundskeepers, the head honcho in the dining room, waitresses, yacht club attendants and car jockeys for their expensive wheels.

Peter cruised down to the Royal Palm Yacht Club and parked in the employees' lot. At the main dining entrance were several young men in liveried white shirts and blue shorts, standing around a valet desk. An older man with thin wisps of grey hair covering the tips of his ears appeared to be in charge. As Peter had once worked as a valet, he knew how the system worked. The oldest of the group was "The Man" who hired, fired, took a percentage of tips, and knew everything about every member of the Royal Palm Yacht Club.

The golf course and clubhouse were being renovated, so activity seemed centred on the dining room. Although it was only the beginning of the season, Peter was able to secure a part-time position to work on weekends. He presented himself as reliable, unlikely to steal loose change from members' cars—exactly what the boss man wanted.

With discreet questioning, Peter confirmed that de Sa was an extremely wealthy man—and a good tipper. De Sa had been a member for over ten years, came from South America, and spoke Portuguese. Rumour connected him with everything from Columbian cartels to white slavery. It all seemed a little far-fetched, but something had to support that lifestyle.

Jose de Sa drove a Bentley. His wife, a drop-dead beauty named Xiomara, drove a red convertible Beemer. Although Peter guessed de Sa would be in his late seventies, Xiomara was no older than forty. He made a point of parking her car as often as possible, and each time she tipped him ten dollars—an hour's wage at the bank. These people had bucks.

Aside from security, Peter wondered if the gold coins were squirrelled away in safe deposit boxes for a reason. Was de Sa hiding them from the IRS, or was it drug money? The coins were dirty, Crawford was absolutely positive, and they were about to become his. Greed has a power that clouds all reason.

If he could steal them, chances were that the theft would never be reported to the police, putting the proverbial cat among the pigeons. But Peter knew that didn't mean he'd be free and clear. He'd have to make himself scarce very quickly.

Luckily, Peter's father had been an American citizen married to a Canadian. The family had moved to the States when he was eight, before his father died of a massive stroke. As a result, Peter carried both Canadian and American passports. After his father's death, his mother sold their Fort Lauderdale house and moved to Canada, to the Ontario tourist town of Bracebridge where she'd grown up. Peter had gone with her and his father's insurance policy provided the money to pay for his Commerce degree from the University of Western Ontario. He hadn't been a great student. Dissatisfied with his prospects in Canada, Peter returned to Florida where he eventually found entry-level work at the bank.

If he could successfully relieve de Sa of his gold, dual citizenship would be integral to his disappearance. Peter Crawford could be in Canada before the old man even knew the coins were missing. And a million bucks would go a long way toward paying for the life he knew he deserved.

The old man had taken a liking to Peter. On his monthly visits he made a point of waiting, even when Peter was busy. He always needed help with the deposit boxes, of course, but de Sa was a man of few words and the few he said were barely understandable. With a lot of concentration, Peter could make out what he was saying. This pleased the old man a great deal. He always ended his visit with a formal handshake and a pat on the bank employee's shoulder. One day the rich bastard confided excitedly that he was going to Portugal on vacation for a month. De Sa wouldn't be back to the bank until mid-August.

Peter had to rein in his euphoria. How fortuitous! He had a month to carry out the next phase of his plan. This was no time to make any dumb moves.

GOLD & GREED

1

IAN MURDOCH pushed out from the ladder and kicked his legs. August was proving to be a hot month and the surface temperature of the lake was bearable. He knew, however, that if he went down more than three or four feet it would be like swimming into a deep freeze.

Lake Muskoka was always like that. At the north side of his island the depth was an incredible 150 feet. When he and Caitlin had fished for lake trout off the point, if they ever caught one, it was ice cold when they reeled it in.

The swimming, part of the therapy ordered after doctors pulled a bullet from his leg, was working. In just over a month, Ian had already stopped using the shillelagh Matt Finnerty had loaned him. He could now walk with only the hint of a limp and, if he was careful, very little pain.

Alone on his island during this first week of August, Ian was making a second attempt at the vacation his boss had ordered. It was, Matt Finnerty insisted, what his mind and body needed. Even so, the nightmares of being wounded in a shootout were never far away. Caitlin never left his consciousness, of course, but that wasn't a "feel-sorry-for-yourself" remorse. It was more a silent companionship, like a warm hand on the small of his back. In September it would be a full year since doctors had warned them the end was near.

Jean Musgrave, on the other hand, was a more recent and painful memory. Every time he shook the stiffness out of his leg he was reminded of the price exacted by poor choices.

Ian heard the pounding of a Boston Whaler hitting the waves as it approached Sea Gull Island. Turning to the sound, he immediately recognized both people in the boat. Albert Cowan, from the marina, was a regular visitor, but the second man was a surprise.

"I'll be damned."

Albert threw a line and Ian pulled them close. The passenger, an older man, first tossed a gym bag onto the dock and, with Albert's help, struggled to get out of the bobbing boat. Finally, he sat on the dock and swung his feet onto the planks. Ian, using both arms, lifted him to his feet before thanking Albert and offering him twenty dollars. Albert, uncharacteristically, refused.

With full throttle, the Whaler was soon gone and the two men were left staring at each other. Ian was first to speak.

"You look like shit, Dad."

"Thanks, Ian. You're pretty pathetic, yourself."

"What the hell are you doing here?"

J.T. Murdoch simply shrugged, a gesture Ian was too familiar with, and offered no reply.

"What's with the bag? I hope you're not thinking of staying overnight."

"Now wait a minute, Ian. I know you've no use for me, but I need to talk to you. Matt Finnerty told me how to get here." Ian's father paused to catch his breath. "He also told me the whole story of how you were shot. Whether you know it or not, I've been keeping tabs on you over the years."

"Remind me to tell that Irish bastard to stay out of my personal life. What's gone between us is strictly between us. Neither he or the Force have any damned business in my private life."

"Just a minute, son. The OPP has nothing to do with this. It's strictly between Matt and me. He even wanted to call you, but I wouldn't let him. I knew you'd just tell me to go to hell. The only way I could get to talk to you was have Albert Cowan bring me here unannounced. So I gambled that you wouldn't throw me in the lake."

"You're damned lucky I don't. The only reason I won't is because I know you can't swim. I'm not going to be charged with murder for the likes of you."

"Look, Ian, I've wanted to say something for the last five years. If you won't listen to me, call Cowan's to pick me up. First, though, indulge an old man. I have to use your bathroom."

Ian took a closer look at his aging father. He looked awful. Damn the old bastard, showing up out of the blue and wanting to talk. If he'd spent less time drinking and a bit of more time talking all those years ago, none of this would be necessary.

"The cottage is open—second door on the left." Ian picked up his father's bag and followed his halting progress up the path.

A few moments later, J.T. Murdoch was standing in the living room, staring up the lake towards Bala.

"This is a beautiful place. You and Caitlin must have spent

a lot of wonderful times here." J.T. paused for a moment, as if deciding whether to proceed. "You know, I went to the funeral. But I stayed out of sight."

"That's a hell of a lot more than you did for your own wife," Ian spat back at him. He could feel the hair on the back of his neck stiffen. "How in God's name could you do that to her?"

"That's what I'm here to talk about. You know, Ian, it'll be eleven years tomorrow when your mother walked out on me. It's like yesterday, it's still so vivid in my mind. We were living in that old apartment on Close Avenue in Parkdale. She walked into the kitchen with two suitcases and just said, 'I'm leaving you, John Thomas.' When she was mad at me, she always called me John Thomas. 'Don't try to find me,' she told me. 'I've had enough of you and I don't want to see or speak to you ever again.' And she was right, she never saw me again for the rest of her life."

Ian didn't want to have this conversation. Certainly not here or now, but there was no avoiding it. Something was bugging the old man.

"You can't believe she decided to leave on the spur of the moment. And it's not like she conspired with us. I never knew she was going to do a thing until I got the call, wanting to know where she'd gone." Ian took a deep breath as the memory of his sister's phone call rushed back. "It wasn't until a week later that Mom called Maurene to tell her she was all right."

Both men grew quiet, watching the lake and letting the fire of their argument subside. J.T. Murdoch had never spoken with his son like this. In fact, Ian thought he'd probably never confided in anyone like this in his entire life.

"When you and then your sister married and moved away," the old man began, "the glue that held us together as a family was gone. I started to drink a little more every day, not just on weekends."

"A little?" queried Ian.

"Okay, a lot. I was scared, I was fifty-seven and we were living from one paycheque to another in a rented apartment, getting deeper in the hole every year. I was too far over the hill to get a decent job and I hated the one I had. I knew I could get fired any day. The booze wasn't helping."

The elder Murdoch continued to stare at the lake surrounding them, relieved that the serenity of Sea Gull Island allowed him to unburden himself. "Yes, this is a beautiful place."

Ian put a kettle on the gas stove, a spoonful of instant coffee in cups for each of them, and waited for the water to boil. He watched his father shift uneasily in the chair. Afternoon sun flooded the room, illuminating his father's face. God, he wondered, had it really been eleven years since they'd seen each other.

J.T. looked a lot older than his sixty-eight years. He had the mottled, grey complexion of someone seriously ill. Caitlin's final months had taught Ian to recognize the signs. He waited for his father to continue as he poured the water.

"I was so wrapped up in my own miserable life, I had no sympathy for your mother," J.T. confessed. "She was hurting, too. I know that. She'd had enough of a man who was going to hell in a hurry with a bottle in his hand. I didn't have the guts to face reality.

"She just packed up and left. And you know something,

Ian? It took me a long time to realize it, but she did the right thing. I was a selfish, weak bastard. If I'd been more understanding, we could've worked our problems out and made a new life for ourselves. She knew me too well, though."

"Have you had anything to eat today?" Ian asked.

"I had breakfast at a greasy spoon in Gravenhurst this morning. Coffee'll do me for now," J.T. answered.

"You'd better stay the night, then. I'll take a couple steaks out of the freezer and we can eat out on the deck. If you want, I'll take you into town tomorrow. We can go out for dinner with a good friend of mine."

Thankfully, Ian's father shifted the conversation to small talk—construction of the cottage, the seclusion of island life, and small, unremarkable events. Eventually, he reached into his pocket and placed a small item on the kitchen table.

"That's my five-year medallion from AA. My group gave it to me at last month's meeting. I haven't had a drink in five years, if you can believe it. I can remember, as if it was yesterday, when I finally made up my mind to quit."

Ian picked up the bronze coin. It felt warm in his hand. Embossed on the face was the Alcoholics Anonymous emblem, his father's Christian names, John Thomas, and the inscription "5 years August 2004" on the back. He looked into his father's eyes, paler than he ever remembered them. He could see pride and accomplishment there, a look Ian couldn't remember seeing since he'd been a kid.

"I was under a building," his father continued. "Some kind of a construction shack down on the Toronto waterfront. I remember crawling in there to die. I don't know how long I'd been drunk, but I'd reached a point where I was certain I was going to cash in my chips. I wanted to hide away where no one would find me. When I woke up, the morning sun was shining. It was so bright I was sure I'd died and was about to meet my maker. I don't know how long I lay there before I eventually realized I wasn't dead. How stupid does that sound? I decided then and there that I had to stop drinking."

Ian palmed the AA medallion, watching his father intently.

"I don't know how, but I got to an AA meeting on Yonge Street. I stumbled in the door and collapsed. A sponsor took charge of me. I owe that man my life. He got me to a hospital and, when I was able to get around, found me a job as a dishwasher. It was exactly what I needed. I stood over a hot dishwashing machine, sweating all of the poisons from my system. I attended an AA meeting every night with my sponsor, and gradually I got my head straight. Thank God."

"When did you cross the line, from an occasional, mean drunk to an alcoholic?" Ian asked.

"When your mother left. I hated her for leaving after all those years. How could she do that? Well, I know the answer to that, really. But I was mad all the time. The company had enough of me, so they fired me. I drifted from job to job, ending up a derelict on the streets. I can't tell you how many times I wound up in the Don Jail. I'd been beaten, robbed. One time someone even stole my shoes. I was at the end of my rope when I crawled under that construction shack."

J.T. excused himself and went to the bathroom again. When he returned he was pale and nervous. His hands were shaking.

"One of the twelve steps in the Program is to make amends

for all the harm I've done," he explained. "I've hurt just about everyone I ever loved. I talked this over with my sponsor and he said I should ask you to forgive me. So here I am, asking you to forgive me for all the cruel and insensitive things I did to you and your sister, and especially ask you to forgive me for not going to your mother's funeral. I knew she'd died, and I knew where the funeral was being held and where she was to be buried. I couldn't face it without one drink to steady my nerves. I'm sorry, Ian, but like so many times before when I had to face a difficult decision, I didn't have the guts to make it. I escaped down the neck of a bottle."

"Being a police officer," Ian interrupted, "and especially with the job I have, there's a lot of stress. It isn't an easy thing to handle. I know several good men who've become alcoholics. I can understand why they end up drunks or commit suicide. But you had a good job. A loving wife and family that adored you. What in hell was your excuse?"

"I've no excuse, Ian. Alcoholics never know when they cross the line from a social drinker to a person whose life is consumed by the only thing that matters—getting that next drink. I know it sounds cliché, but one drink isn't enough and two is too many." J.T. wandered out to the deck.

The steaks had thawed enough to fire up the barbecue. The two men, father and son, watched the RMS *Segwun* as she sailed silently round the point of Sea Gull Island. J.T. couldn't get over how close she was. He waved at passengers standing on the upper decks of the historic steamship, and the captain obliged his greeting with three blasts of the whistle. J.T. laughed for the first time since he arrived.

Ian noticed softness about his father's eyes and felt a warm stab of recognition. It was a feeling of admiration, perhaps even love. Ian couldn't accept the sensation. A stronger sense of abandonment and resentment overpowered the fledgling emotions. He put them out of his mind, a habit he'd acquired since Caitlin's death.

"Now that you're sober, what are you doing with your life?"

"Well, I told you about my sponsor. When I finally understood the AA philosophy, and got my life in order, he gave me a job. He owns a numismatic business. You know, he buys and sells rare coins, out-of-circulation paper money, that sort of thing. Even has a website that connects with buyers and sellers all over the world. He specializes in coins. It's nothing for him to do a hundred thousand dollar's business in gold in twenty-four hours."

J.T. Murdoch shifted his position at the picnic table. Ian could see that he was in pain and hesitated, unwilling to ask about his discomfort. Soon the old man continued.

"It's a very interesting business. There's a network of coin dealers that belong to an association—a very exclusive club. They all know each other and, above all, there's complete trust in every transaction between them. If a dealer in Italy has a buyer for South African Krugerands and my boss has them, the transaction takes place over the Internet. The money gets wired and the coins are shipped immediately. Both dealers stand to make a profit.

"My sponsor's a wonderful teacher. He gradually brought me along so that I'm a fairly knowledgeable coin merchant. I'm not in his league, but he trusts me with the day-to-day buying and selling over the counter in his store. When there's a big sale or purchase, I always turn it over to him. Like I said,

Ian, he saved my life. I'm not telling you that it's all hearts and flowers. I have times when remorse almost consumes me. For now, however, I have my AA meetings and I even sponsor several other people who are alcoholics just like me. I'm not successful with everyone, but it's a great feeling when someone makes it. I speak at meetings where I tell my story, simply and truthfully. It gives purpose to my life."

After eating, Ian collected their cutlery and dishes. From the kitchen he could watch his father sitting peacefully outside. J.T. had become an old man, much older than his years. The alcohol had taken its toll, of course, but there was something else. He'd eaten only a small portion of his steak, blaming his lack of appetite on a greasy breakfast. It was obvious that there was something seriously wrong with him. As hard as it was to shut the last eleven years out of his mind, he couldn't stop loving the old bastard. Not for the first time since Caitlin died, Ian resisted the urge to cry.

The breeze shifted to the southwest, mosquitoes moving to the calmer air in the lee of the cottage. J.T. could no longer stand the torment, although he was reluctant to leave the dying light of the setting sun. The expanse of water between island and mainland had transformed into a tapestry of shimmering gold. When he noticed Ian watching, he simply smiled and repeated, once more, "God, this is beautiful."

"You look tired. I've cleared the junk out of the spare bedroom so you can bunk in there."

"The air here has a way of catching up with you," J.T. admitted. "It's impossible to keep your eyes open."

"Sleep as long as you want tomorrow. We won't go into town until after lunch."

It seemed a waste to sit in the dark on Sea Gull Island. Ian flopped half-dressed onto his bed. The only sounds were his father's muffled snoring and the click of nighthawks snatching abundant insects from the cooling air. In the morning, daylight would creep stealthily across the island. Nature was still hours from lifting her grey blanket of mist when Ian awoke to find his father shaking his arm.

"There's someone out on the lake hollering for help. Come outside, you can hear it."

Ian slipped into shoes and joined J.T. on the deck. From the northeast point of the island a cry could be heard. Without a moon in the ink-black sky, nothing could be seen across the water. He found his searchlight and hurried to the corner of the island nearest to the frantic sound, waving its beam back and forth on the calm surface of the lake. He searched in sectors, the beam travelling farther and farther out into the night. At last the stark light picked out a stilled boat. An unidentifiable person frantically waved and shouted.

"Help!" The voice barely carried over the distance. "Help!"

Ian flashed the light to acknowledge the request, then hurriedly threw on a T-shirt and jacket before going to start up his boat. Without asking, J.T. put the kettle on, anticipating that whoever was out there would appreciate a hot drink. Ian said a silent prayer and his own motor started with one pull. Wonders will never cease. He steered toward the voice and eventually located it once more with the light. On the water, at the same level, it was even more difficult to pick out any object.

"Oh, God, am I glad to see you. I've been shouting for an hour." A grateful young man shivered in the damp night air.

"Thank you, I thought I was stuck here until morning. And the flies have been eating me alive."

The panic-stricken young man couldn't stop babbling. "Those damned flies are vicious. Are you from the mainland or one of the islands?"

"Easy now. If it wasn't for my father hearing you yell, you would've been here until tomorrow morning." Ian attached a line from the stern of his boat to the bow of the younger man's, explaining as he worked. "I'll tow you over to my dock for now—I'm just about a half-mile away on Sea Gull Island. I'll call Albert Cowan in the morning and he can tow you to the Marina."

Ian took a moment to look over the stranded boat, marvelling that he'd even seen its dark hull or the young man's darker clothing. The battery had obviously been drained trying to restart the engine, leaving no power for the running lights. There was no sign of flares having been used, and no evidence that there'd ever been any on board. A single life jacket lay discarded on the deck.

"You know, it's against the law to be out without proper safety equipment. You should at least have a flashlight and whistle." The police officer's voice of authority always seemed present with Ian.

"I just bought this boat and trailer down the highway, near Orillia. The guy said it was in good working order. He never told me there wasn't any safety equipment. Then the damned thing just quit as I was heading towards Rankin Island. I fiddled with it for hours before the battery went dead. Then I was afraid one of those cigarette boats might come by and slice me in two. I've seen it happen in Florida."

"You weren't too swift, taking a new boat out at night. Why didn't you wait until morning?"

"It was still daylight when I launched in Gravenhurst. Our family's had a cottage on the east side of Rankin Island for years and I was so anxious to get there I'd forgotten how far it was. I guess I didn't think clearly."

"I guess not," Ian growled impatiently. The least the young bastard could do was offer to help, but he seemed content to sit back and be rescued.

At the dock, Ian tied his own boat then secured the young man's craft behind it. J.T. met them with a Coleman lamp and led the way, holding the lantern high so they could see the rocky path.

The kettle was whistling as the three entered the inviting warmth of the cottage. The young stranger, tanned and good-looking, put out his hand to the elder Murdoch.

"I'm Peter Crawford," He said. Finally he turned to Ian, for all the world like a king in his manor. "And to who do I owe my rescue?"

2

IT HAD BEEN THE SECOND TUESDAY of the month and, like clockwork, Jose de Sa entered the bank. Peter had been ready for him, pretending to be busy at his desk. He looked up, feigned surprise, and indicated he'd be right with the rich old bastard. This was it, phase two. If the scheme failed he was dead in the water.

Peter had laughed to himself, deciding his hands weren't shaking any more than de Sa's. With the old man leaving for Portugal, this was his chance. Now or never, he'd thought.

The bank always supplied two client keys when renting a safe deposit box. Instructions were that one should be kept in a safe place while the other was used to access the box. The bank maintained a master key, although it was only for the first of the two security locks on each box. The master key was inserted, triggering a mechanism that allowed a customer's key to unlock the individual steel doors. Clients could take their box to a secure room and privately remove or deposit whatever they wished. It wasn't unusual for people to store money, jewellery, heirlooms and, as Peter was convinced in Jose de Sa's case, gold. When finished, they were replaced in much the same manner. Both client and bank keys were required to secure the box in its own vault.

Because his diseased hand shook so badly, the old man couldn't easily insert his own keys. Over time, as trust had built up, he began giving them to Peter to unlock the boxes. Finished in the secure room, he always called for Peter to return them once again, using both keys. Peter had planned carefully, timing and rehearsing every move.

On the day Peter made the switch, de Sa's treasures had been replaced. Peter gave the old man two keys, as usual, but this time they were from different boxes, ones whose locks had been drilled for various reasons. De Sa wouldn't be able to open his boxes again with those keys but, if he'd followed the bank's instructions, he still had another set that would.

The old man had concluded his visit that day just like every

other, with his usual handshake and a pat on the shoulder
for Peter. "I'll see you in August-a," he croaked in his thick,
heavy accent.

Afterward, Peter sat at his desk, hiding his own hands so
that no one could see their tremor. Operation Gold Mine, as
he'd privately nicknamed his plan, had begun.

A camera in the vault room recorded everyone entering and leaving the area. In a separate room opposite was a
cabinet housing videotape of each twenty-four-hour period.
Elsewhere, more cameras monitored every facet of the bank's
life. It was part of Peter's job to change tapes for the camera
watching the drive-through ATM. The machines for both the
vault and ATM sat on adjacent shelves in the security room.

It had taken very little conniving to change the routine,
under reasonable pretence, to Tuesday evenings. Peter was
counting on the tellers being too busy balancing their cash
to witness his movements.

That evening he'd pressed the stop button on both VCR's,
even though he was only authorized to operate the less sensitive ATM monitor. Slipping quietly into the vault, he used the
bank's master key, turning it quickly to allow de Sa's keys to
be inserted and unlock the boxes. When he'd lifted the lids,
he thought later, it was a wonder his heart hadn't stopped.
Both were full of clear envelopes laid one atop the other and
lined with glimmering coins. There were, quite literally, doz-
ens of them. But Peter had no time to stare.

Heart pounding at the possibility of discovery, he put the
boxes back into their respective vaults. In the end, it was
hard to remember not to run as he returned to the security
room. He hit "start" on the vault-room machine, and then

inserted a rewound tape in the ATM monitor as usual. Apart from a missing few moments of tape that stood little chance of being noticed, there was no record of anyone entering the vault. The whole procedure had taken all of two minutes, but it was another four tension-filled days before both boxes were empty. At the beginning of the following week, barring any security breaches, the vault-room tape would be rewound and taped over.

One factor Peter hadn't fully appreciated was the weight of the coins—almost thirty pounds in total. It was probably the sheer weight that made him fully conscious of their value. Even if coins proved difficult to exchange, thirty pounds of solid gold was still worth something. He became paranoid, but waited until there could be no suspicion as he sweated out the long, painstaking days until he felt comfortable giving his manager two week's notice.

The two-bit apartment he lived in was about as safe as an open-air flea market. His first hiding place, under the mattress, lasted only two days. The next was the freezer of his refrigerator where the coins took up far too much space. He then settled on carrying them around under the mat in the trunk of his beat-up car, enduring nightmares of being rear-ended and coins spilling all over the road. He'd begun to appreciate old de Sa's reasons for inspecting the coins every month. For a kid who'd never had more than a couple of hundred dollars in his pocket, holding a small fortune wasn't something he was equipped to handle. By the time he'd given notice at the bank he was a nervous wreck. Once, he even considered returning them. Greed soon chased that thought from his mind.

Every night he had examined the coins. There were 175 twenty-dollar Liberty pieces, 84 South Africa Krugerands, 112 Austrian Philharmonics, 126 Canadian Maple Leafs, and a variety of others from the United Arab Emirates. Some were Swiss and there were several whose origin he couldn't decipher. All were a single ounce of pure gold and, as far as he could ascertain, in mint condition.

Peter had estimated the current value of the Liberty coins at approximately $350,000. Searching the Internet for everything he could find on the rest, he learned that the Maple Leaf was legal tender in Canada and could be sold for the price of its gold. They'd be easy to move when he got to his destination.

The coin business, Peter had soon discovered, was very complex. There were coins that traded worldwide on the open market, their value predicated on the Precious Metal Exchange in London, England. Then there were out-of-circulation coins whose value was tied directly to the quality, age and the purity of the sample. The twenty-dollar Liberty was one of those, quoted on-line at $1850 U.S. per coin.

On Peter's last day at the bank, the manager had treated him to lunch and assured him there was always a job waiting if he ever returned to Florida. Peter was certain that would never happen. When de Sa found that both Peter and the coins were missing, it wouldn't be long before he put two and two together.

One thing Peter knew was that rich people seldom acquired their wealth by being stupid. Certainly, de Sa would come after him, and to disappear into thin air wouldn't be easy. He'd read that people operating on the dark side of society had methods of tracing people that even the FBI would envy. He hoped that spreading the rumour he was going to California would be sufficient to keep his final destination a secret. Unfortunately, "the best laid plans of mice and men gang aft a glee."

Driving up 1-95 then 26 East to Columbia, South Carolina, before following 77 and 79 North, Peter had gotten as far as Morgantown, West Virginia, before checking into a motel. Exhausted from worrying that his shit-box car would crap out and strand him with its cargo of hidden coins, sleep still eluded him. He parked directly in front of his motel room window and begun to doze off, only to leap out of bed to see if the car was still there. He didn't dare unload the coins, having carefully spread them out flat on the floor of the trunk and glued the mat back down. Besides, all his worldly belongings were thrown on top. The effort needed to remove them would attract unwanted attention. No one would suspect such a beat-up car with all that junk to be carrying a million dollars in gold coins, he told himself to no avail.

He had a million dollars in cash. And, he kept reminding himself, that was a conservative estimate.

The next major hurdle had been crossing the border from Niagara Falls, New York, without being searched. Since 9/11, security had grown tighter than ever. He had debated which passport to show, deciding on the American. He was driving a car with Florida plates, after all.

The line-up on the Canadian side of the Rainbow Bridge allowed Peter to mentally rehearse for Customs and Immigration. Finally at the booth, an officer asked the purpose of his trip. Peter handed over his American passport, saying he was vacationing in Muskoka for two weeks. He tried to remain as calm as possible, hoping his body language wouldn't trigger the officer's curiosity. The last thing he needed was—

Peter's stomach nearly dropped through his rectum when he was instructed to drive to the inspection area. A dozen horrific scenarios flooded his mind, perspiration running freely down his back. He had to get himself under control. Fortunately, it was another twenty minutes before anyone else approached.

A young female officer asked why he'd been directed to the inspection area. Peter had admitted he didn't know—he was simply going to visit his mother in Bracebridge, Ontario, for two weeks.

"Would you please open your trunk, sir?" She stepped away from his car as she made the request. "Are you bringing any gifts, liquor, cigarettes or firearms into the country?"

"No. No liquor or cigarettes, and I don't own a gun." Peter had answered honestly. "Just what you see. Enough for a two-week vacation in Muskoka."

As the officer moved his folding travel bag, the corner of the mat came with it. Peter had to steady himself on the fender, knees buckling.

"All right, sir, have a pleasant stay in Canada," the uniformed girl concluded. "And enjoy Muskoka. I hear it's beautiful there."

He'd wasted no time closing the trunk, driving out of the parking area and onto the road leading to the Queen Elizabeth Way. A few kilometres later he stopped on the shoulder, feeling nauseous, his hands shaking. If he'd known Operation Gold Mine was going to take such a toll on his nerves, he'd never have started it. He was over his head, in unfamiliar water, but he was quickly learning to swim.

After regaining control he'd pulled back into traffic, headed for Toronto on the QEW. His first priority had been to sell a handful of Miss Liberty coins to a dealer on Yonge Street. Then it was up the 400 and north on Highway 11. He could hardly wait until he reached Weber's to buy something to eat. It was a tradition his family had always observed.

Disappearing wasn't so hard after all, he'd mused. He couldn't stop smiling.

3

A CROW WOKE IAN, cawing for its mate from a birch tree outside his bedroom window. Young Crawford was stirring in the kitchen, likely anxious to call the marina. He could wait. No one at Cowan's moved until eight o'clock and it was still only seven, the beginning of a hot August day. There wasn't a cloud in the sky and the lake was as calm as a millpond.

Peter had certainly made himself at home. The aroma of percolating coffee was inviting. Ian was slightly annoyed that the kid had taken such liberties, but let it pass without comment as he entered the kitchen.

J.T. had already taken a mug of coffee down to the dock where he'd settled under an umbrella at the picnic table. Ian and Peter soon joined him. Later they spoke with Lori, Albert's wife and co-owner of the marina. Someone, she said, would be out for Crawford's boat within the hour.

During their conversation over breakfast, Ian wondered

why Peter Crawford, for all his gregarious nature, said very little about himself. Murdoch's years in the OPP, and specifically his homicide training, told him this kid was running away from someone or something. At the moment, it wasn't his business. All he wanted was to get him off the island. Crawford was beginning to annoy him, constantly going to his boat, pacing the dock, and asking repeatedly when the guy was coming to tow him in. It was a beautiful craft, even if the engine didn't run, but it wasn't so great that it deserved getting quite so worked up over.

Finally the familiar sound of Cowan's Boston Whaler could be heard rounding the point. Albert turned the motor into a sharp curve, cut the throttle, and washed into the dock on his own wake. He'd lived on the lake all his life, and no one could handle a boat like Albert. He quickly hooked up the towline and was off, up the lake, taking Crawford with him.

"That smart ass was beginning to piss me off," Ian told his father. "He never shut up, but he never really said anything, either. There's something strange about him."

"You said it," J.T. concurred. "You know, he got up at least four times that I heard last night. Kept going down to look at his boat. There was no damned wind, last night. Was he afraid it was going to drift away? He had enough ropes on it to hold the *Queen Mary.*"

"Enough of that jerk," Ian laughed. He then became immediately serious. "I've been looking at you and you don't look healthy. Are you going to tell me what's wrong, or will I have to call Matt Finnerty? He seems to be the one you confide in."

J.T. Murdoch's response didn't really surprise his son.

"I have prostate cancer. I was diagnosed a year ago and I've been taking these new, experimental injections. So far it appears to have the cancer under control, but I go back to Princess Margaret next week for tests. What they've been telling me is that you can have prostate cancer for years and it won't kill you. At my stage in life, the ravages of old age will get me before the cancer does."

Ian paced until his father lost patience with him.

"For Christ sake, sit down. You're worse than young Crawford."

"Don't try to pass this off as something that won't kill you, I know better." Ian glowered at his father. "I watched Caitlin go through hell for the last three months of her life. I'll make sure I get the facts straight from the horse's mouth. When's your appointment?"

"Next Friday. I can't remember the time, but if you give me that cell phone number I'll let you know." J.T. looked relieved at the concern in Ian's voice.

The two men sat quietly for a while, adjusting slowly to their new relationship. Finally, J.T. broke the silence. "I've pretty much said everything I wanted to say. Why don't you take me into Gravenhurst and I'll buy you lunch. Then you can put me on the bus to Toronto."

"I'm not going to tell you that all is forgiven, J.T. There's a lot of hurt that needs to come out. Christ, eleven years just can't be swept away overnight, and we're not getting any younger. After my own close call last month, I've had to do some soul searching. I guess what I'm saying is that I want you to be a part of whatever life we have left to us." Ian wrote his cell number on a business card and stuffed it in his father's pocket.

On the way to town, Ian thought they might as well check with Albert at the marina, make sure that he got the kid's boat going. Albert waved them over to the gas pump. He was filling the tanks of a launch and Ian marvelled as numbers flipped past on the pump's face. When they hit the $190 mark, Ian stopped watching. He looked to J.T.

"Man, am I glad I don't own that gas guzzler. I thought my puny twelve-horse was expensive to run, but two five-gallon tanks doesn't seem so bad after all."

"Thanks for sending that Crawford guy here." Albert guided them to the shade of the boathouse. "If you find another like him, though, send him some place else. That son of a bitch is completely bananas. I hooked up the charger and still couldn't get the damned thing started. Then, when I told him I'd have to put it in the shop he went ballistic. There was no way he wanted that boat in the shop."

Ian and J.T. shared a look, remembering Crawford's strange behaviour during the night.

"I told him, either I put her in or he gets it to hell out of my marina. He finally agreed, but he stood watching over my shoulder the whole time like he had the crown jewels hidden in there. So I charged him for a new battery, two coils, and four hours labour at the full rate. He paid cash with American money, which amazed me. Didn't blink an eye. Usually those assholes bitch like mad and then pay with a credit card."

"Do you know him?" Ian asked. "He said his family has a cottage on the east shore of Rankin. Must've been anxious to get there to try to take a new boat over at night. If J.T. hadn't heard him hollering, he'd still be floating around out there."

"I think I remember him from years ago. He was just a kid when his father died, but his mother has family in Brace-bridge and she came back to Muskoka. We used to open their cottage in the spring and close it up in the fall when they lived in Florida. His mother has a boyfriend now. When he's around he looks after the place for her."

Another boat pulled into the fuel pumps and Albert had to run. Leaving his own boat in its slip, Ian walked with his father to the parking lot where his car was stored. They opened the doors to cool the car down before getting in.

While they waited, he punched a number into his cellular phone. He hadn't spoken with Edna Walters for nearly a week and it would be a good opportunity to see how she was managing.

"Edna," he began without preamble when she answered. "How would you like to have lunch with my father and me today?"

"Oh, gosh, Ian. Today's my Penny Bingo day and I've baked my special carrot cake for the gang. They'll be expecting me. Why don't you come over to my new apartment after your lunch and have dessert and coffee with me. Bingo's over by three-thirty, if that's not too late for you. I'd love to meet your father and I'll even save some cake for you."

"Sounds great. We'll see you then."

Driving into town they stopped for construction at the new Wharf project. Ian tried to explain some of the plans for the property. As they waited alongside an enormous formation of Precambrian stone being blasted away, Ian pointed to the water where three "pods," the fashionable name for condominiums, were to be built and sold for anywhere from three to six hundred thousand dollars. Nearby were sites for a new hotel, a heritage centre and restaurants. Heavy equipment was busy driving piles near the shoreline, giant quills on an imaginary porcupine's back.

It was impossible to picture how the project would end up and Ian quit his attempt at description in frustration. By then, summer traffic was once again moving and they proceeded on to Sloan's Restaurant for lunch. He almost ordered their famous blueberry pie until J.T. reminded him that they were going to Edna's for dessert.

The new apartment building, where Edna had purchased her two-bedroom unit on the ground floor, was within walking distance of the Senior's Centre. Edna was at the front entrance when Ian and J.T. arrived.

"Mr. Murdoch," Edna gushed. "I can see where Ian gets his good looks."

Beaming with pride, Edna Walters ushered them inside.

"I had an interior decorator from Bracebridge help me pick out the furnishings. What do you think, Ian?"

Ian looked around, noting the entertainment centre with a wide-screen TV, stereo, DVD player and the works. Edna was taking full advantage of her settlement from the estate of Werner Richter, the late prisoner-of-war-turned-millionaire and father of her son, James. Given the circumstances of James' death, Ian couldn't begrudge the new life she justly deserved. He put his arm around Edna's shoulders, admiring the designer chic straight from the pages of some glossy magazine.

"Edna, I'm proud of you. You've rejoined the world and look like you're thoroughly enjoying it."

The three of them sat in the comfortable living room, enjoying strong coffee and Edna's famous carrot cake with crushed pineapple. J.T. and Edna made small talk like old friends until it was Ian's turn to remind his father that the bus to Toronto left in only twenty minutes.

Before leaving, Edna made Ian promise to return soon, perhaps for dinner. For his part, he wondered aloud why he'd worried about her fitting into her new world. Edna was just getting used to the formalities of entertaining after almost sixty years of reclusive devotion to her murdered son. She'd adapted wonderfully well and it was one worry lifted from his mind, quickly replaced by concern for J.T.'s health.

Ian waited with his father at the bus station in Gravenhurst. Just as J.T. was getting on the coach he shook hands with Ian, then tried putting his arms around him. Uncomfortable with a public display of affection, the son left his arms at his side. The bus driver, witnessing it, raised one eyebrow to Ian in admonishment. Before he could change his mind, J.T. had turned and waved as he went up the steps to find a seat.

"Shoulda given him a hug," the driver whispered. "He isn't getting any younger."

"Yes," Murdoch admitted. "I wish I had."

Ian parked in front of the Community Policing building next to the post office. Although he was technically on leave, he couldn't break the habit of checking in. Sure enough, there was a message from Matt Finnerty. The boss wanted him to report to Orillia the following Monday at ten. Very formal, Ian thought. What did that Irish bastard want now?

Ian had two days to relax before he'd meet with Finnerty, but there were a hundred chores to do around the cottage. Winter played hell with a seasonal building in Muskoka, and being on an island multiplied it by ten. It would be nice to finish just one of the chores before summer was over. He decided to start by fixing the gas water heater. One of these days he was going to take an axe to that piece of shit. He vowed that if he ever got the sixty thousand dollars to bring an electrical cable to the island, he'd do it.

The piddling jobs kept him busy all day. His only relief was a short break when the Royal Mail Ship *Segwun* sailed silently by. The murder of Edna Walters' son, James, and the role the *Segwun* had played in solving it, had made Ian a bit of an eccentric hero to the crew of the beautiful old lady. The captain always gave Ian three languid blasts on her steam whistle when they passed Sea Gull Island. Whether he liked it or not, Ian and his island had become part of the lore of Muskoka.

4

IT WASN'T THE SECOND TUESDAY of the month, but Jose de Sa and his young wife arrived together to perform his usual routine. Unable to check the contents of his safe deposit boxes, his holiday had seemed an eternity. When he'd finally returned home, the first thing he wanted was to see his beloved coins.

At the bank, he asked the manager for Peter. When told he was no longer an employee, de Sa was initially disappointed. The manager went with them to remove the boxes from the vault. This time it was Xiomara who inserted her husband's key. The tremor in the old man's hands was quite visible now, perhaps exaggerated by anticipation of the moment.

Of course the key wouldn't turn. And, when she inserted the key in the second safe deposit box, it wouldn't turn either. She tried switching the keys but it made no difference.

The old man became very excited, mumbling to his wife in a language the manager didn't understand. She placed both keys in her husband's shaking hand and he tried to insert them himself, to no avail. Finally he blurted a string of words only she understood, but their meaning was clear enough. It was obvious that both Mr. and Mrs. de Sa were very upset. Xiomara advised the fawning manager, in perfect English, that they had brought the wrong keys. She apologized, and told him they would return the following day. It may have been the manager's imagination, but he thought the old man practically ran from the bank.

In the parking lot, Jose and Xiomara sat in the Bentley for a long time. People who live on the questionable side of the law are neither innocent nor naive. Quickly, de Sa had concluded his keys had been switched, and that Peter Crawford was the only one with the opportunity to do it. "That son of a bitch," he spat in Portuguese. "He's stolen my coins."

Back in Royal Palm, de Sa retired to his office to consider.

His first priority would be to locate Crawford. It was certain he wouldn't be anywhere in South Florida.

"Go to the Yacht Club," he ordered Xiomara. "Talk to the young guys that park the cars. These kids gossip all day long. He might have tipped his hand and told someone where he'd go."

This move at first produced very little. Xiomara caught a group of car jockeys doing nothing, and they all thought Peter had gone to California. He'd quit his job at the bank, sold everything, and was driving across country, as far as they were aware. To disappear in a big state like California, she knew, would be very easy. She was ready to leave when one of the young men came to her, motioning for her to open her window.

"That's what Peter told the guys," he smiled, hoping to make an impression on the beautiful trophy bride. "I think he was going back to Canada, though. He told me once that his mother lived in some big tourist area north of Toronto— Bracebridge. I remember the name because I was getting my partial bridge fixed by the dentist at the time. I'm sure of the name. She has a summer home on an island, he said, but he could have been shittin' me."

Xiomara pushed a twenty into his shirt pocket. She couldn't wait to tell her husband, in person, just to see how far his own generosity would go. Jose was on the phone in his office when she returned. He waved her in and motioned for her to sit. Normally she would never have entered his office when he was on the phone. She'd learned that lesson early in their marriage. She knew very little about the nature of his business, but she had her suspicions. Lately, with the onset of Parkinson's, he was relying on her more and it was an involvement she didn't want. She married Jose de Sa because he could afford her and he needed a beautiful woman to hang on his arm. The fact she spoke Portuguese was a great advantage to them both. Her American mother had always spoken English, but her father had spoken several languages, including his native Greek. Since childhood, languages had come easily to her.

Her mother had brought her to New York from Greece when she was seventeen, after a very bitter divorce. She'd been educated in the best of schools, graduating from Vassar. For several years she'd been content to live on looks instead of intelligence, modelling in New York, London and Paris. But she didn't like the hectic pace or the occasional switch-hitting, drugs, and depraved parties with demanding millionaires that came with the fast life.

One winter, while on a photo shoot in West Palm Beach, she was introduced to Jose de Sa at a cocktail party. He saw in her the china doll he'd always dreamed of, and she saw a meal ticket for life. Certainly there'd been affection, as well. She'd never have gone through with it if she hadn't at least some admiration for him. Although nothing had ever been put to paper, both knew exactly what her position was. At least, that's the way it had started. With the progression of her husband's disease he began to involve her increasingly in what she guessed was a dubious business.

Jose de Sa had always been secretive. She knew he'd had a previous wife, and most likely children, in Brazil. It hadn't been a concern, at the time. And whatever he'd done to accumulate his wealth wasn't her concern, either. When they met, he was a U.S. citizen, living in the very best community in Boca Raton. He belonged to the Royal Palm Golf Club, had a big yacht docked in the back yard of a house worth four million dollars, and was prepared to spend lavishly for her company. All she wanted in return was to live her life—golf and tennis lessons, shopping, lunch with the girls, and A-list invitations in Boca Raton and New York.

Beyond advertising his wealth, Jose de Sa didn't give a damn about any of this. His young wife and their beautiful house, all the trappings of a multi-millionaire, none of this could compete with the obsession that had been the centre of his entire life. The only thing that meant anything to Jose de Sa was money. He never played golf or went out on his boat, and only watched TV for the stock quotations. What Xiomara and her continual parade of male guests found funny on reruns of Seinfeld left him cold and disinterested.

The removal of his precious coins lit a fire in Jose de Sa that consumed him. They were his first love, the culmination of a life's work, and he had to hold them, count them, constantly admire them spread on a table at the bank. He'd take them out of their plastic pouches to rub his thumb and forefinger over their surfaces. It's why he went to the bank every second Tuesday of every month. And now they were gone. When he thought how easily a simple bank clerk had duped him, he couldn't control his rage. He'd get his coins back and that young bastard, and whoever else was responsible, would pay with their lives.

5

IT WAS A NORMAL MONDAY MORNING at Ontario Provincial Police headquarters in Orillia. Matt Finnerty was at his desk by seven-thirty as usual, a habit he couldn't break. The rest of the brass opened for business no earlier than eight o'clock. Matt had been on the receiving end of snide remarks about his early start ever since he'd begun to move up in the ranks, but he'd ignored them all. He never admitted to using that precious half-hour for quiet thought, his golden time of the day.

The phone rang, disrupting his reverie. It was an outside line, one that few people had access to. The voice on the other end came as a surprise.

"John? John Alcorn, why the hell are you calling at this time of the morning? You're in Orillia? Sure, come right up to the main entrance and reception will direct you. Better yet, I'll have someone meet you there."

Matt sieved through papers on his desk, selecting any of a confidential nature and sliding them into the top drawer. He puzzled at the call, wondering how Alcorn had got his direct number to begin with. Alcorn was chief legal counsel for the Police Commission in Toronto, and a heavy-hitter of the first degree. It shouldn't be hard for a guy like that to have access to a lot of things. But Matt was shocked the call had come so soon. He had, after all, only put out his first timid feelers on the weekend. Alcorn was wasting no time.

John Alcorn didn't bother to knock, opening Finnerty's

door and walking straight in. Matt leaned across his desk and offered his hand.

"Glad to see you, John. How long has it been—five or six years?"

"More like eight, Matthew. You haven't changed. More snow on the mountain and an inch or so on the gut. Other than that, you look great."

Matt smiled but didn't return the compliment. He didn't have to because, as he well knew, nothing he could say would improve Alcorn's opinion of himself. John Alcorn was an obnoxious asshole, but an effective lawyer. Tall and gangling, he had a long, thin face that could contort into the most frightening expressions at will. His famous shock of black hair, thinning slightly, was turning to salt and pepper at the temples. A new streak of silver running from his widow's peak to his crown added to an already commanding and eccentric presence. Alcorn slouched into Matt's swivel chair.

"I spent the night at the Casino. The hotel, I mean. My wife received a voucher for a free meal and accommodation so she bugged me until I agreed to come along. I left her at the nickel slots and took a chance on reaching you." Alcorn's gaze tried to penetrate Finnerty's impenetrable façade. "We have to talk."

Here it comes, Matt thought to himself, steeling for the moment.

"Don't get your balls in a knot, Matt. I wanted to tell you I'm putting your name forward for the position of Chief of Police for the Metro force. You can expect to be added to the short list."

"That's got to be the hottest potato in Canada for a cop."

Matt shifted uneasily in his chair. "What makes you think I'd take the job even if it was offered?"

"You and I go back a long while, Matt. You are, first and foremost, a good police officer. And I know you're a clever political animal. You'd be perfect for the position." Alcorn let a smile edge across his face. "You've survived the political machinations of the OPP, for one thing, and that in itself gives you the experience to handle both the politicos and the press in Toronto. Last, but not least, I owe you."

Matt was trying very hard not to register any emotion. "You've caught me completely by surprise with this, John. That's one position I hadn't thought of aspiring to. Not quite yet, anyway."

"Oh, come off it, you big leprechaun." Alcorn's smile widened dangerously at Finnerty's evasion. "You and I both know you'd jump at the chance to be top cop in Toronto—in all of Canada, for that matter. You can lay that unconcerned Irish bullshit on people around here, but I know you too well."

"I'm afraid there's one strike against you." Alcorn's mood changed abruptly. "It's come up at a couple of review meetings."

"And?" Matt inquired, although he already knew the answer.

"You're too close to your officers. The committee members have some misgivings about whether you'd be able to handle the Police Union. In Toronto it's all-powerful, and if you can't control it, you can't run the show."

"Bullshit." Matt was now standing at the corner of his desk, visibly annoyed. "I get the maximum out of my people. Every man and woman in my department puts out a hundred and ten percent for me. And it's precisely because I know every wrinkle in their personalities and exactly how to motivate them."

"And Ian Murdoch?" Alcorn asked from beneath his raised eyebrows. "Talk is that you're covering up for a trigger-happy inspector."

"What's that supposed to mean?"

"It means that one of the committee members has a cottage in Muskoka. Word is that the story in the newspapers isn't the real one. The cottage cocktail circuit is all abuzz with rumours that you covered for Murdoch when he went on a spree at Muskoka Wharf, endangering civilians as they disembarked from the *Segwun*." Alcorn waited for a reaction that never appeared before upping the ante. "And then, they say, you hushed up the shooting death of one of your own officers."

Finnerty raised an eyebrow, as if daring his visitor to continue.

"Word is, Matt, that he deliberately disobeyed your direct order and left the hospital to pursue a suspect. And that, they say, cost an officer her life."

"You know something, John? You can take my name off your list. If your committee gets its information from the gossip circuit, then I don't want anything at all to do with them."

"Don't get riled, Matt. I'm only telling you what one person said at a meeting. I can handle that kind of negative crap, and so can you. I'm not going to take your name off the short list. I want you to be top cop in Toronto."

Matt couldn't afford to let Alcorn's comments about Ian Murdoch go unchallenged.

"Do you know that Murdoch is the best detective in the entire OPP? Do you know he solved a murder while shutting down the kingpin of the biggest kid pornography network in Canada?"

"Alleged kingpin, Matthew. It hasn't been proven in a court of law, yet."

"Well, we're far from finished with the list of prominent people who were customers of Frank Airscliff's website. By the time we're done, it'll have international implications. Ian Murdoch brought a three-year investigation to a head, and there are a few citizens in Toronto who must be crapping their drawers as we speak. Believe me, John, this investigation is not going to be swept under the carpet."

"No one is asking you to sweep anything up, Matthew. However, you might consider how involved you want to be, and your friendship with Murdoch. Making waves isn't going to land you the best and biggest available job in your profession." Unperturbed, Alcorn stood and walked to the door.

"Matt, I want you as the Chief of Police for Metro Toronto. I know you want the job, and I have complete confidence that you can do it."

Alcorn reached out his hand, almost as an afterthought as he left the room, and Matt shook it. It was the kind of handshake that careers were based upon. Alcorn made a show of checking his watch.

"I've got to get back to Rama and pick up the Missus. She's probably already blown the hundred bucks I gave her. Christ, and it isn't even nine o'clock. You know, she comes up by bus every month and gets a free meal ticket for the Casino. All the money and advantages I've given her over the years and she spends her time gambling with a bunch of immigrants. That's a pretty sweet cash cow for the government, isn't it?"

The lawyer didn't wait for Finnerty to reply. He was out the door and on his way before Finnerty had a chance to speak. Instead, the big Irishman reclaimed his swivel chair and faced the morning sun as it streamed through his window. Less than fifteen minutes before it had been a relaxing position. And then along came John Alcorn with an offer to become the chief of Canada's largest municipal police force. Had this always been what he'd worked toward? Whatever the reason, it was there in front of him. He was being considered, was actually on the short list.

Matt Finnerty closed his eyes and smiled to himself.

6

IT ONLY TOOK THREE CALLS to locate Mrs. Isobel Crawford. Xiomara made the last one, as her husband had instructed, explaining that she was from the Boca Raton bank Isobel's son had worked for in Florida. The bank, she told Isobel, needed an address to forward Peter's final paycheque. After the call, Xiomara left Jose's office as quickly as possible. She had no appetite for what she knew would follow.

Jose de Sa had obvious connections in the gold coin business. He'd used one specific dealer in Boca to buy coins for many years, and that dealer had a computer link-up with every legitimate dealer in the world. He also wasn't averse to a bit, or a lot, of cash on the side, having grown very adept at hiding transactions from the Internal Revenue Service. Armed with a list of the stolen coins, de Sa's dealer put out a "buy order" for any available amount of the various denominations. As well as the United States, the request went to all major dealers in Canada. The old man knew the kid would have to sell something soon, if only to get money to live on, but it was still a surprise when word came back that Liberty coins were already on the market in Toronto. They'd been purchased five days before, at a bargain price of thirty thousand Canadian dollars. The old man went into a fit of rage, hurling a thousand Portuguese curses to the heavens.

There was no possibility of monitoring every dealer in Canada but, unless the kid went nuts, thirty thousand bucks would last him for quite some time. Toronto was only a two-hour drive from the town where Isobel Crawford lived. He'd have to go to Bracebridge, de Sa decided, and find the little bastard. When he recouped the remaining coins he'd kill the son of a bitch. And he had to do it fast, before Crawford was tempted to sell anything else.

He had a name, he had a town and, with his wife's help, he had an address. Peter Crawford was about to pay for his arrogance. But Jose de Sa couldn't do this alone. Neither his health nor his command of the English language was adequate to operate on his own in Canada, especially in some small Ontario hick town. Fortunately he had a plan, and he had Xiomara.

A frequent visitor to the de Sa home in Boca was an old and trusted friend. Orby Lintz was a veteran of Vietnam, reporting for duty on his eighteenth birthday, long before the fall of Saigon. After the war he took work as a bodyguard, first for a Texas oil magnate and then others. De Sa had met the Texas wildcatter on an oil lease deal in the Orinoco River Valley of Venezuela where he'd been operating as bag man for the local government. A minor government official had interrupted an oil lease to an American company. Mr. Lintz managed to eliminate any objection to completion of the deal when the fledgling tycoon supposedly blew his own brains out. De Sa made a lot of money. He hired Lintz, of course. He was Jose's "go to" guy.

Mr. Lintz lived on the twelfth floor of a South Ocean Drive condo overlooking the Atlantic. Word amongst the resident divorcees and widowers was that he'd retired from a successful career as a financier. It was a fiction that suited his habits perfectly. He spoke several languages fluently, devoured cheap novels, and quietly belonged to an exclusive gay club in South Beach, Miami.

Now in his late fifties, Orby Lintz looked forty and had a muscular physique that younger jocks would die for. Jose de Sa suspected that some may have done just that. Yet he wasn't conspicuous, travelling more or less unnoticed. For all appearances, Lintz was simply another weary businessman. The fact that he'd left whatever conscience he'd begun with in an Asian jungle permitted him to do what was asked with proficiency and dispatch. For two hundred thousand a year, plus completion bonuses, Orby Lintz remained at Jose de Sa's beck and call.

Orby Lintz sat with the old man, smiling grimly, as de Sa

instructed his Boca dealer to place a buy order for all twenty Liberty coins that had surfaced in Toronto. A few hours later they were on their way to Toronto where Jose grudgingly paid cash to recoup his own property. Old man de Sa flew directly to Toronto with Xiomara and Lintz, all on the same flight but with Lintz travelling separately. Lintz surreptitiously carried the money for the coins—crisp, new American money that created quite a stir with the Canadian dealers. Each of the hundred-dollar bills was individually examined with an illuminating pen that ensured none were counterfeit. The three hundred separate American bills, even with the exchange, provided a tidy profit for the dealer.

Xiomara and Jose de Sa had immediately travelled north. They rented their own car and two suites at an exclusive Lake Muskoka resort in Gravenhurst, just a few miles from Isobel Crawford's home. Lintz left them in Toronto, following a separate itinerary and booking into a budget hotel in Bracebridge. All three carried brand-new cell phones and cards from a Canadian distributor, with numbers programmed for speed dial. Jose de Sa was adamant that they keep in touch, but speak only in Portuguese as an added precaution.

After dinner, Isobel Crawford took a telephone call while watching television. The very soft-spoken man was polite but insistent. He was a lawyer, he claimed, representing the estate of one Jamison Crawford of Hamilton, Ontario. There was a considerable sum of money left to surviving family and he was certain Mrs. Crawford was one of these lucky relations. It was the oldest scam in the book, but Orby Lintz knew people always believed in money when they doubted everything else. Mr. Michael J. Thompson wondered if he could visit Isobel Crawford, at her house, and verify that her late husband was indeed a relative of the dear, departed Jamison.

An hour later it was a very excited Isobel Crawford who welcomed Orby Lintz into her living room. He carried a bulging briefcase and looked exactly as she imagined a lawyer should if he was about to write a cheque for untold fortunes. First, Mr. Thompson wondered if there was anyone else in the apartment and, by the way, didn't she have children? The answers were no and yes, and she told him about her only son, Peter.

"I'd like to speak to Peter when I discuss the estate with you. Is that possible, Mrs. Crawford?" Lintz inquired.

"Whatever you have to say, I can tell him. In any case, Peter isn't here." Isobel was becoming belatedly suspicious. Thompson was making her nervous. She could sense that something was wrong.

"Mrs. Crawford, as a potential heir, it's imperative that I also speak to Peter. Where is he?" Lintz was opening his brief case.

Isobel walked towards the front door, fully intending to usher Michael Thompson from her home. Lintz was across the floor like a cat after a mouse. With a movement that was almost intimate, he placed one arm around Isobel's shoulder while the other went around her neck, a hand clasped firmly over her mouth to prevent her calling for help.

"If you make one sound, lady, I'll twist your head clean off your body," he whispered in her ear. He gave her head a jerk to reinforce the threat. Isobel Crawford urinated through the fabric of her best dress.

Dragging her to the kitchen, Orby Lintz took a roll of duct tape from his case and wrapped her to a kitchen chair. He tore off two more pieces, long enough to cover her mouth. Isobel Crawford was totally confused, frightened out of her wits. What was going on? This lawyer didn't want her, he asked only about Peter. What had Peter done now?

Quickly and silently, Lintz checked every room in the apartment, making sure the front door was locked. When he returned to the kitchen he calmly pulled up a chair and sat facing Isobel, tears making rivulets in her makeup and the stench of piss emanating from her.

"Look, Mrs. Crawford, I don't want to hurt you," he spoke soothingly. "All I want is to talk to Peter. I have urgent business with him and, if I can talk to him today, right now, I'll be on my way. Then neither you or Peter will ever see me again." Lintz leaned closer. "Now, why don't you just tell me where your son is and I'll cut you loose."

She shook her head violently, perspiration flying from her hair. Her eyes were wide, full of fear, staring into Lintz's own, eyes completely devoid of emotion. She knew that he was lying to her, that he'd never cut her loose. Oh God, what had Peter brought down upon them? What in God's name had he done to make this monster suddenly appear?

Lintz went to his brief case and removed a pair of pliers. The price tag from a local hardware store was still attached. Gently taking her left hand, he placed the jaws of the vice-grip on her index finger, set it to the proper thickness, and began to close them.

Isobel's body writhed in unbearable pain. Her eyes shot open wider, tears running down her cheeks. She couldn't stop her head from flailing back and forth. Lintz calmly whispered in her ear. "Where is Peter?"

She stopped thrashing long enough to refuse his request. With each refusal he repeated his sadistic act, occasionally on a new finger. Twice, she fainted. Twice, Orby Lintz revived her so that she could experience the full force of his persuasion.

Lintz was growing more impatient with every squeeze of the grips. Finally, when she fainted a third time, he slapped her face, his ring raking a deep cut over her eye. Blood ran down her cheek. Frustrated, he grabbed her shoulders and shook hard, the chair rocking on the kitchen floor and Isobel's limp body flopping like a rag doll.

Her head falling forward, she gave a muffled groan as she expelled the air from her lungs. Her brain, starved for blood, cried out for the life-giving liquid. Every organ of her frail body hungered for a share of the depleting blood flow dissipating from a ruptured artery into her brain cavity. Her sphincter relaxed and the nauseating stench told Lintz that she'd soiled herself. Isobel Crawford's life came to a sudden, convulsive end as her punishment induced a massive stroke. Lintz couldn't have known that doctors had warned of this possibility a full three years earlier. He searched frantically for a pulse, lifted her eyelids and listened at her chest for a sound.

"Goddamn you, you bitch. Goddamn you."

Lintz walked the floor, repeating his curses over and again. With the old broad dead, there had to be something else in the apartment that would give him a clue, help in locating Peter Crawford. She was his mother, for Christ's sake. He went through everything in the living room, but found nothing. In the bedroom he found only a photograph, Isobel and Peter sitting on a cottage dock. On the reverse, in a proud mother's hand, was written "May 02—Rankin Island." He put the photo in his pocket, leaving the building as silently as he'd come.

Orby Lintz wasn't an amateur, although he cursed his amateurish loss of the old woman. He remembered the information Xiomara de Sa had obtained from the car jockey about a summer home on an island. Rankin Island, he now suspected as he drove down Manitoba Street, the main thoroughfare of Bracebridge, to a combination bookstore and art gallery. Catering to a summer clientele, it was still open after eight in the evening. There he bought a vinyl map of the Muskoka Lakes, returning to his car to inspect it. He smiled, letting the speed-dial ring through to Jose de Sa. Orby Lintz knew exactly where to find Peter Crawford.

7

IAN STUFFED HIS BLUE TIE into his blazer pocket, zipping them both into a plastic suit bag. His grey slacks and pale blue shirt would be okay until he arrived at the OPP lot in Orillia. That would be soon enough to finish dressing. Unconsciously, he reached for his service weapon, and then shook his head in disbelief. Old habits die hard, and he wasn't used to reporting to work without a holster nestled familiarly against his body. He felt naked.

His weapon, of course, was already at headquarters. It had

been there ever since that long weekend in July when he'd been forced to use it. He hadn't missed it before because he'd been on leave, recuperating from the wounds he'd received from Wolfgang Richter and Frank Airscliff, two major investigations that had come to a fatal head within hours of each other. All weapons fired, resulting in injury or death, were taken immediately for examination by the Special Investigations Unit. Ostensibly, it was to preserve evidence in the event of legal action, but Ian wondered if they hadn't been taking just a little too long in announcing the results of their deliberations.

The old boat motor was its usual unpredictable self. After failing to start on the first few attempts, he caught the whiff of gasoline as the carburetor flooded. He waited for ten minutes, then fired it on the fourth attempt. Dropping it into an idle, Ian loaded his extra gas cans, garbage, empty water bottles and clothes into the bow of the old aluminum boat. No sense making two trips when one would do. He'd drop everything off at Cowan's and Albert would take care of refilling the gas and water before he returned. The garbage would go into an "Island Residents Only" container in back of Albert's shop where the casual public wouldn't be tempted to fill it up.

Before letting go the lines, Murdoch stood on his dock and gazed wistfully across the lake. Muskoka is beautiful in August, when the weather cooperates. Cottagers and tourists had long since settled into enjoying the dog days of summer, and even the prospect of murderous Friday and Sunday migrations up and down the Gaza Strip, Highway 400, could not seem to deter them. That morning, as Ian lay awake thinking of Caitlin, he'd heard the plaintive call of a loon for its mate. The distant response had pierced straight to his soul. For the longest time after, he simply stared at the ceiling. It had been four years since Caitlin had painted the tongue-and-groove pine boards, getting as much paint on herself as on the ceiling. Another winter and they'd need painting again.

He'd dragged himself out of bed, leg aching and stiff, to make coffee. Ian Murdoch could not allow the black dog of depression to return. As usual, his solution was activity.

Out on the lake, he circled the island once before heading to Cowan's. In the lee of Sea Gull Island it was calm, the trail of his twelve-horse the only disruption. Across the shimmering water, on the town side, he could see the swell of fast boats pulling kids on bloated tubes and the crest of a skier's waves breaking the mirrored surface. The morning sun reflected on their wake as they darted and twisted in the distance. Over their familiar whine he could hear the delighted screams of kids. Looking back, he smiled at the mirage presented to him. If not for the rocky shore of his island it would be impossible to distinguish sky from lake.

Halfway across, Ian undid his sweat-soaked shirt and let it flap in the breeze to dry. It was hot already, damned hot, and perspiration irritated his injured leg. By afternoon, the exposed western side of Sea Gull would be like an oven. Maybe it wasn't such a bad day to spend in an air-conditioned interview room, after all.

According to an early morning call from Finnerty, it was a simple formality. Special Investigations, or SIU, were expected to give their long-awaited decision on events surrounding the shooting of Wolfgang Richter, following which the Superintendent would hand over files on the death of Jean Musgrave. Ian's own account would be reserved until after review of the files. He was, technically, a witness, even though it had been that bastard Airscliff who pulled the trigger. The former lawyer and pornographer had been formally charged with Jean Musgrave's death, as well as the earlier murder of a former lover. Edna Walters' daughter-in-law had died decades earlier, to be honest, but Frank Airscliff was still every inch a killer.

Further charges regarding the sexual abuse of minors, and purveyance of child pornography through an internet network of like-minded people, were pending. Ian didn't know much about that end of things and he didn't want to find out. The probability of finding photographs of an adolescent Jean Musgrave was enough to make him physically ill.

Ian hadn't really spoken to Finnerty about Airscliff's arrest or the hours leading up to it, but he had confidence in his Superintendent. Matt wasn't the kind of guy to let the truth get in the way of a good story, but he'd never let down members of his command.

At headquarters, a receptionist directed Ian to Conference Room B on the second floor where, she assured him, Mr. Finnerty was already waiting. Ian checked his watch, discovering that he was fifteen minutes early. In Room B there were actually four men awaiting him. Matt sat quietly in a corner and only nodded, while Graham Huff was having a polite conversation with Ian's union representative, Bill Watts. Huff was familiar from previous Special Investigations interviews, a reasonable enough kind of guy with the grudging respect of the troops. The fourth guy, however, was a stranger. A stranger wearing a five-hundred-dollar suit. He introduced himself as Roland Lavallee, special counsel to siu, whatever that meant.

As the microphones and recorders in front of the men were checked and rechecked, Ian detected a hint of accent in Lavallee's speech. Northern Ontario French, if he guessed correctly. Murdoch wondered what it was about the man that seemed familiar, but gave up as Graham Huff called the interview to order.

Huff, as chairman of the inquiry, read the siu findings into the record. Two forty-five-calibre bullets had been removed from the body of Wolfgang Richter. After due investigation, it had been determined that both were fired from a weapon retrieved and identified as belonging to Inspector Ian Murdoch.

"Further," Huff continued with apparent relief and satisfaction, "it has been determined that Inspector Murdoch fired his weapon in self-defence and out of concern for the safety of innocent bystanders. Accordingly, no charges will be laid and, in light of events that transpired, I hope his commanding officer will make appropriate comment in the Inspector's personnel file. Inspector Murdoch may pick up his property from the Arms Control Store after he fills out the appropriate paperwork."

Huff looked to Finnerty and actually allowed a hint of a smile to cross his face. That was allowable—smiles wouldn't be heard on an audio recording.

"Perhaps, Superintendent, some sort of commendation might be in order. That's entirely up to you, of course."

Finnerty nodded. His concentration focused on Roland Lavallee.

"I guess that's it for me, then." Bill Watts spoke. "You won't be needing my representation for the rest of it, will you Ian?"

"Thanks for coming, Bill. We're good to go." Ian shook his rep's hand as Watts made a hasty exit from the room, duly recorded by the chairman. The door had barely closed behind him when Roland Lavallee spoke.

"I'd like to deal with the death of Constable Jean Musgrave, at this time, gentlemen." He looked directly at a surprised Ian. "Could we begin with you, Inspector? I'd like you to relate, in as much detail as possible, your version of events preceding the fatal shot by Frank Airscliff, and everything that has transpired following that moment."

Ian was caught off-guard. This wasn't how it was supposed to go. First the paperwork, then the interrogation. Any preliminary questions should have been directed to Matt, as senior commanding officer. Murdoch hadn't even been conscious for much of the time in question. Finnerty had the reports from all the officers involved, and he should have been fielding any questions. Even then, the reports should be officially turned over first and reviewed before any questioning.

There was no way Ian could dance around direct questioning. Had Matt Finnerty set him up? No, Ian decided, both Matt and Graham Huff seemed to have been sandbagged by Lavallee's new direction.

There was a gentle knock at the door. A young woman, dressed in the casual business attire of an aspiring detective, asked for Superintendent Finnerty, then whispered in Matt's ear when he joined her. Finally he returned to Ian and his interrogators.

"I'm sorry to break this up, gentlemen, this is Detective Sergeant Janna Logan. There's been a body discovered in an apartment in Bracebridge. Sergeant Howard, the local staff officer, suspects foul play. He wants to know what detectives I have available, and unfortunately that's Ian. I'm going to have to borrow Inspector Murdoch for a while to help out Sergeant Logan."

"I thought the Inspector was on a disability leave," interrupted Lavallee.

"Well, in that case he shouldn't be required for further questioning."

Matt Finnerty motioned for Ian to follow him. As far as he was concerned, the meeting was over. Logan trailed behind as they left the room and Ian wondered why he'd never heard of her before. Matt asked Logan to bring them up to date as they took the elevator down.

"Yes sir. It's pretty obvious that it's not accidental. Her name's Isobel Crawford, late fifties, lives with a boyfriend in a reputedly quiet apartment building. All we know so far is that there weren't any reports of disturbance and Lou is securing the scene until further instructions."

"Any sign of the boyfriend?" Ian interjected.

"Not yet, but we're about to start looking."

"Do me a favour, Ian. Don't turn this into a public shooting gallery like the last one. This time, Logan is the lead officer and you're just along for the ride. I'm getting enough flak about you without being accused of letting a senior officer on a medical disability take control of an investigation. You'd better get up there right away." Finnerty stepped aside and let the elevator doors glide open.

"So much for August medical leave." Ian stepped out of the elevator, dumbfounded. He wondered what the hell was going on. First a meeting that was inexplicably hi-jacked, then being pulled out for an investigation that he wasn't even going to be in charge of. Why in hell would Finnerty make him play second fiddle to a female detective that he hadn't even heard of before? For a moment, he considered telling the Irish bastard to go screw himself. Murdoch could easily go back to his island and spend his time doing nothing constructively.

"Beats the alternative, Ian. Don't bother showing up around here again until everything's squared away." Finnerty didn't directly mention Roland Lavallee, knew that he didn't have to. Matt watched carefully for signs of a limp as his oldest friend made his way out of the building. It was there, but Ian was hiding it well.

"Just a minute, Janna. Before you go, I'd like a private word."

The young officer looked at her boss quizzically, but followed his lead as he stepped back into the elevator.

"Is everything all right, sir?"

"No, Sergeant. Everything is not all right. And that means I've got a job for you, above and beyond the normal investigation." Finnerty sized Logan up, deciding she'd have to do. "You may or may not know that Inspector Murdoch has recently been injured in the line of duty. You might also know that he was instrumental in bringing Frank Airscliff in, although it was a little premature in my judgment."

"Yes, sir. Pretty much everyone's heard about the shootings."

"Let's dispense with the 'Sir' routine, for the time being. Under the circumstances, I think you can call me Matt, or just plain Finnerty, like that disrespectful son of bitch you're going to be working with." If he hadn't smiled, she might have been tempted to take his tone of voice seriously.

For the next few minutes, Finnerty briefed Logan on her additional assignment. She was to keep an eye on Ian, involving him as much as possible in the investigation without relying upon him and, above all, watch out for anyone who might try to undermine him. What puzzled Janna Logan most was Finnerty's inference that someone was trying to discredit Murdoch, portraying him as a Dirty Harry, a rogue officer.

He emphasized that Murdoch's unconventional methods had quickly and intuitively solved the murder of Gravenhurst accountant James Walters, although it had almost cost him his life. Walters was the illegitimate child of a German multi-millionaire who, near the end of his days, had decided to leave him his vast fortune. Unfortunately that led his only legitimate son, a spendthrift criminal, from Europe to Canada on a wild spree to kill off the competition.

Murdoch's hunt for Wolfgang Richter had been sidetracked by the coincidental discovery of the body of James Walters' former wife, and the fact that a prominent local lawyer had once been her lover. Frank Airscliff became a chief suspect, and there was only one reason Finnerty had left him at large. Jean Musgrave had spent her entire law enforcement career collecting enough evidence to bring down the man who had sexually abused her, as well as the rich vein of pedophiles he'd been procuring for.

Finnerty left out mentioning that Musgrave's actions in the final few minutes of her young life may have been construed as complicity with Airscliff. That was a secret known only to Finnerty, Murdoch and Howard—and they'd do everything in their power to protect her memory. It was enough, Matt thought, that Logan knew certain wealthy and influential people were trying to cloud Airscliff's prosecution. They didn't give a damn about Murdoch. Their only concern was ensuring the trail didn't lead back to them.

"If Ian's involvement in this case can be used to undermine the prosecution of Airscliff, why don't you just pull him back out?" Logan asked. She tried hard not to let her own ambition leak into her voice, but Finnerty didn't care.

"Because we need to catch a killer. Unconventional or not, Murdoch can help you."

"Is that the only reason? There must be other people who won't cross the line."

"Maybe," Matt admitted. "But Murdoch's a damn good friend and an even better cop. He's recently lost his wife and a young partner. I'm not going to take away one of his last reasons to get up in the morning. Work with him, Janna. Pick his brains and, above all, keep him safe."

That said, Finnerty released the elevator doors and set her loose on the world.

8

MURDOCH DROVE WEST on Highway 12 before merging into the northbound lanes of Highway 11. He was crossing the Severn River before he remembered his firearm, still in the OPP Stores. If he hadn't been so preoccupied, remembering how outspoken Caitlin could be when facing down bureaucracy, he would have retrieved it when he had the chance. A quarter of an hour later, at well over the speed limit, Ian turned onto Muskoka 118 to Bracebridge. His cell phone buzzed. It was Lou Howard with directions to an apartment near the town centre.

One thing Ian appreciated about Lou was that he always used his head. He'd been on the force long enough to avoid contaminating a crime scene. Ian was sure he'd have the apartment sealed and the immediate area taped off. Ian and Lou had known each other since high school, and although they never spoke of it, for all those years they had shared a secret. In this profession, Ian mused, a secret should follow you to your grave. This one had already outlived at least one person.

His thoughts returned to the moment. Had it been just a fluke, or had Matt Finnerty instigated SIU's questioning? Probably not, especially since he took the first opportunity to get Murdoch out of the building. Just the same, something wasn't right.

"We've got to stop meeting this way," Lou Howard greeted him when he arrived.

The apartment building was on a street leading to the hospital. Ian had spotted two cruisers outside and the telltale yellow tape restricting access. He'd grabbed his bag from the backseat and retrieved his camera and notepad, handy for everything from bird watching to investigating a homicide. Lou had been waiting for him at the main entrance to the building.

"Her name's Isobel Crawford," Lou continued. "She worked at a local bank but when she didn't show this morning a friend called her apartment. No answer, so the bank manager eventually called the building manager. After repeated attempts to contact her, he opened it up about an hour ago and found her. So far, nothing's been touched. The super hightailed it as soon as he saw her and I haven't even been beyond the front door. That's far enough until the experts are done."

"You haven't had a doctor in to pronounce her?"

"Didn't need to. You'll see for yourself that there's no hurry. I thought the technical people could finish their work, then the doctor can move her as much as he likes."

Before entering the apartment, Ian put on the white paper suit that a constable offered. He checked his camera for film, took a deep breath, and stepped through the doorway. At first there was no sign of struggle. All the furniture in the living room appeared to be in place and the visible rooms were neat and tidy, with the exception of Isobel Crawford's body, in plain view from the front entry, fastened to a kitchen chair with duct tape.

There was a double strip of the silver adhesive across her mouth. Her arms were by her side, drawn to the back of the chair and held fast with more tape. Her head hung to the side, mouth gaping, eyes open. There was a slight cut on her left eyebrow, a trickle of dried blood on the cheek and traces over the tape covering her mouth. Isobel Crawford's face was contorted into a horrific grimace and there was obvious discolouration. Ian walked cautiously around the body, searching in vain for a wound. Nothing apparent. He'd have to wait for Forensic to make the call. In the meanwhile, he decided to look around the rest of the apartment.

Behind its closed door, the bedroom was a shambles. Drawers had been emptied onto the floor and clothing and papers lay in heaps everywhere. Home invasion? Robbery? Murdoch didn't think so. Perhaps someone had been searching for something. What, he wondered, would someone like Isobel Crawford have that would be worth her life?

Sergeant Howard was standing in the kitchen entrance. Ian asked if the coroner had arrived and Lou motioned outside where a figure was struggling into a monkey suit. He was the same young doctor who had been to Sea Gull Island a month earlier. Although it was obvious the victim had been dead for some time, his routine check for vital signs had to be done. The smell of voided bowels was sickening. And those damned green flies! As expected at such an early stage, without an autopsy the doctor couldn't estimate time of death any closer than eighteen to thirty-six hours.

Closely monitored by members of the Forensic team, paramedics were waiting for the body. Following interminable minutes of measuring and photographing every detail, Janna Logan arrived on the scene and ensured that the record was complete before authorizing removal of Isobel Crawford's body.

Lou Howard noted her arrival and quickly appraised her.

He'd seen her kind before. The average person could be forgiven for thinking she was heavy, even for her slightly above average height. Her loosely tailored suit, however, was a disguise. It could hide a Kevlar vest or a shoulder holster as easily as the muscular body he suspected she spent long hours in the gym maintaining.

"Lou," said Murdoch. "I'd like to introduce you to Detective Sergeant Janna Logan. She'll be lead investigator on this case."

Lou simply nodded a greeting, keeping his surprise and his questions to himself.

"Sergeant Howard," she responded, before walking carefully around Isobel Crawford's distorted body, taking in as much detail as humanly possible. "I've heard a lot about you and your detachment. So, are we ready?"

Ian cut the tape that held the body to the chair. The full weight of the corpse fell forward onto the kitchen floor before anyone could react. Her left arm spread to the side, hand turned palm upward. Still, Ian noted, there was no fatal wound visible.

Janna Logan looked carefully at the fingers on the body's left hand, surprised to find they were blackened beyond normal lividity, the settling of blood to the lowest point at death. Examination of the right hand showed evident discolouration as well. It wasn't as dark as the left, but Ian made a mental note to check body position in his photographs later.

Logan released the body to the paramedics. She would normally have checked first with her superior, Matt Finnerty, but knew the Irishman was already up to his ear lobes. Besides, it hadn't seemed as if Matt had been anxious to hear from her very quickly. Strange things were brewing.

Logan smiled tightly, already inured to the stench of death that surrounded them, and assigned notification of next-of-kin as Lou Howard's priority. He spent the next few minutes making a cursory inspection of papers in a desk to determine who that would be. Ian found him looking at a picture of a young man.

"Wait a minute, I know that person." Ian didn't like coincidence. In fact, he didn't believe in it. "That's Peter Crawford. He spent the night on my island a few days ago."

Murdoch was relieved that, no matter what Finnerty said, he was now deeply involved in this case. The adrenaline began to pump.

"Her son, maybe?" Logan enquired.

"Well, he said his mother lived in Bracebridge. They've got a cottage on Rankin Island, which is where he was going before he got stranded mid-lake. I hope this isn't what I think, Lou, but we'd better pay him a visit as quickly as possible."

9

ACCORDING TO THE MARINE UNIT, there'd been no sign of Peter Crawford or his boat at the island that afternoon, so Ian and Lou had spent much of the night unsuccessfully looking for additional relations. They'd try again, but first Ian wanted to know just what had killed Crawford's mother.

The autopsy was held the following morning. Ian had temporarily taken up residence at Taboo so that he could be on time for the Coroner's comments. His contrary old outboard couldn't be trusted to start and, anyway, Matt Finnerty couldn't bitch about expenses after his convalescence was cut short once again.

Ian went through the rear entrance of the hospital. Janna Logan was in the examination room when he arrived, watching intently. He found the Coroner already starting his work, the corpse on a stainless steel table with a white sheet over it. A detailed inspection hadn't found any major wounds or obvious cause of death, but they hoped an internal examination would provide a clue. A microphone hung over the table, recording all of the Coroner's remarks.

"The only abrasions found on the body," the doctor intoned, "are to the four fingers of the left hand. The tips of the fingers have been crushed, perhaps by some clamping device, causing severe blunt trauma. There is a small cut over the right eye, superficial in nature. The neck and ribcage appear intact; no broken bones are evident. Neither the wounds found on the fingers nor the head can be considered primary, although they may be contributory to cause of death. In spite of the circumstances surrounding discovery of the body, further examination of vital organs will likely prove my supposition."

The doctor motioned Ian and Logan closer to observe Isobel Crawford's distorted visage.

"The drooping left eye and distorted mouth are indicators. I doubt the injuries were enough to produce trauma of sufficient magnitude, although that's just conjecture at this point in the examination. The condition of the body, allowing for warm weather and the fact rigor mortis had subsided prior to arrival, indicates that death occurred between twelve and eighteen hours before discovery."

Ian had heard enough. He'd wait for the Coroner's written report.

"What's your first best bet, Doctor?" Logan inquired.

"A guess?" The look in his face told Ian that there was no humour intended. "I'd say she was scared to death."

"Okay, Inspector Murdoch," the young detective informed him. "I'll stay until the examination is concluded. I'm very interested in the method of torture used. You and Lou continue with what you were doing, but keep me informed if anything breaks."

Ian thought that Logan was having way too much fun giving the orders for a change. His own job, since Lou Howard had managed to officially confirm relationship, was to tell young Peter Crawford that his mother was dead. Ian had a terrible suspicion that he already knew and Crawford would have to account for his whereabouts. Ian called Lou, requesting a marine unit to pick them up at Gravenhurst Wharf. Meanwhile, he found out from Albert Cowan, who claimed to know every inch of the Muskoka Lakes, exactly where the Crawford cottage was.

When the OPP boat arrived, the young officer driving it insisted Ian put on a life jacket and cinch it tight before leaving the Wharf.

"Don't take it personally," Lou whispered to Ian. "I caught him here with a beautiful young thing without a jacket on. Hell, she was hardly even wearing a bikini, so he's putting the act on for my benefit."

"What's the matter Lou, are you getting that old?" Ian laughed. "I can remember when you were quite a stick man yourself. Is it that long ago?"

Lou ignored the remark, busying himself giving passing boats the "Muskoka Wave," although Murdoch wondered if he was being ignored. Their own vessel abruptly reduced speed to the posted nine kilometres per hour limit as they entered the Narrows. Albert had given specific directions and, once through the Narrows, they headed directly for the east shore of Rankin Island. Ian recognized Peter's boat as they approached the dock. The cottage was set back from the shore, barely visible through a jumble of large boulders and enormous pine trees. At first glance, the place appeared abandoned.

Since the close call on his night run to the island, Peter Crawford had needed time to think. Everything was secondary to the problem of hiding the coins. While at Cowan's he'd bought a heavy-duty plastic tackle box, about the same size as the original safe deposit boxes combined, and the coins fit easily inside. There was no place in the building to conceal the box and the island's shallow topsoil wouldn't permit him to bury it, so he ended up building a rock cairn to enclose it. Winter ice always pushed rocks up on the shore and Peter had spent all of one day lugging enough of them to a secluded spot behind the cottage. The small stone vault he created managed to blend perfectly with the terrain.

Since secreting the coins, he'd been able to sleep through the night without dreams of someone stealing his loot. Still, fear gripped his throat when he heard the sound of a motor. He looked out the picture window and panicked at the sight of a police boat tying up. There were two uniformed officers on board and one man in plain clothes already ashore. He recognized Ian Murdoch immediately. A hundred thoughts raced through his mind. Would de Sa have called the cops? Not likely. He hoped, even prayed, their visit was for some reason other than theft of the coins. Nervously, he walked down the path to greet his visitors.

Ian shook Crawford's hand. He looked directly at the young man when he said, "I'm sorry Peter, but we have bad news. Your mother was found dead in her apartment yesterday afternoon."

Every officer hates to convey such terrible information and Ian was no different. In this case, he closely observed Peter's reaction, ready to judge every expression. Experience had taught him that, if a family member was involved in a death, they often over-reacted. He could sense that with Crawford, but there was something disarmingly honest about his surprise.

Peter's mouth fell open. He staggered, burying his face in his hands and crying openly.

"How did she die?" he mumbled through his hands. "Was it her heart? She had a heart attack a few years ago. Oh, my God. My God, I wasn't there for her."

Ian waited a moment until the young man had composed himself.

"Where is she now?" Peter finally asked.

"There's something else we have to talk about," Ian said. "Can we go up to the cottage?"

Peter led the way, turning to Ian as he walked. "What do you mean, there's something else?" Ian delayed until they were in the cottage before asking Peter to sit.

"There are some facts about your mother's death that need to be addressed. The Coroner believes your mother died of a heart attack, but the circumstances are peculiar. She was duct taped to a chair and it appears she was tortured." Lou, on one side, and Ian both scrutinized Crawford.

"The apartment was in a shambles, and that leads us to believe the motive was robbery," Sergeant Howard added.

"Robbery? She had nothing in the apartment worth stealing. And tortured—what do you mean?" Peter leaned forward in the chair, his hands shaking.

"The tips of her fingers were crushed and she had a cut over her eye. The trauma may have induced a heart attack or stroke. I have to ask these questions, Peter. Is there someone, anyone, you think would harm your mother? And Peter, we'll need you to account for you whereabouts for the last two days."

"My whereabouts? Do you mean I'm a suspect? You should be talking to that leech she's shacked up with. That no-good bastard has beaten her up before, and I can't go near the apartment when he's there. He drives a long-haul transport truck, but when he's not driving he lays around the apartment and drinks. I'll kill that son of a bitch if he did this."

"I'll need his name, Mr. Crawford," Lou interjected. "We'll check up on him. Right now, Inspector Murdoch needs you to answer his questions. Where have you been during the last forty-eight hours?"

"I've been right here ever since the mechanic fixed my

motor. Oh, no, sorry. I went into town, into Gravenhurst, for some groceries yesterday afternoon. Other than that, I never left the island." He turned to stare angrily at Ian. "I resent your questions."

Peter was getting pissed off. In Murdoch's book, that was a good sign. Ian walked to the picture window, the sun at his back so that Peter could see only a silhouette.

"At this point in an investigation we have to suspect anyone who was near your mother's apartment. When you were grocery shopping, did you happen to visit her?"

"No, I didn't. The last time we talked, that lazy bastard was there. There's no way I'm going near Bracebridge when that fucker's around. Why are you questioning me about my mother? Why not go after him?"

"What's his name?"

"Norm. Norm Stokes. He worked for that big transport company in town until they let him go. Now he's a broker out of the city. Owns his own rig and runs her by the mile for anyone that will pay the going rate. These days it's a Just-In-Time company hauling auto parts."

"What time were you shopping?" Ian watched Peter's face. He couldn't tell if it was the sun or if he was actually growing flushed. Crawford was too sensitive, Murdoch thought. He didn't have the hard, calloused attitude of a killer.

"About four? I know I was back on the island by six-thirty."

"If you'll come with us, we'll take you to Bracebridge and bring you back again."

"You'll probably need something else to wear," Lou gently suggested.

"How many times do I have to tell you I was shopping yesterday afternoon? What do you need me for?" Peter was now pacing the room, attempting to shield his eyes from the sun. Suddenly he collapsed in a chair, looking confused.

"Maybe you don't understand me, Peter." Ian was becoming annoyed and added a little official force to his tone. "We'd like you to come with us to the hospital in Bracebridge to positively identify your mother's body. You will put on what clothes you need, and you will be ready to get in that police boat in ten minutes."

"But I can't leave the island."

"Well then, I'll personally kick your ass off the end of that dock and we'll keel haul you up the Muskoka River to Bracebridge. Now move it."

Peter immediately responded to Murdoch's new imperative.

"Look around the kitchen," Ian told Lou. "See if you can locate the cash register slip for his groceries. It should tell us where he shopped, including the date and time. Let's see if the young snot is telling the truth. I'm going to look around outside."

Peter went through an elaborate routine of locking up the cottage as they waited. One good kick to the front door would knock it off its hinges, judging from its appearance. It was an old building but not a classic, probably built in the late seventies with very little proper maintenance ever since Cowans had stopped watching over it. On the east shore of Rankin, it took the full blast of winter storms and they played hell with any building. Ian knew this well, spending days fixing up his own place every spring.

Reaching the mainland, they drove immediately to the

hospital. When Peter was shown his mother's body he gently touched the side of her face.

"Why, Ma? Why? We would've had it good now. I'd have looked after you."

Ian led him into an outer room, catching a quick glimpse of Janna Logan as she left. Logan had been privately watching Crawford's reaction to his mother. Murdoch was impressed. It was the type of thing he would have done himself.

"Are you all right? Can I get you a Coke or coffee?" Crawford only nodded his head. "We've checked with the trucking company and Stokes has been on a run to Chicago. He's presently held up at the Blue Water Bridge in Port Huron, Michigan."

"I don't understand."

"There's no way he was involved in your mother's death. They've got Global Positioning on each tractor and they know where every truck is, every hour of the day."

"But, maybe he left his truck?"

"Sorry." Ian shook his head. "The dock foreman in Chicago has personally vouched for him. He hasn't been back to Muskoka."

A look came over Peter's face that Ian instantly recognized as fear—stark fear. Without waiting, Ian quickly continued.

"You know who's responsible for your mother's death, Peter. Who is it? Now's the time to tell us, before the trail gets cold."

"I don't know who did this." The young man's voice shook with the lie. "I need to go back to my island now."

It was a full ten minutes before Murdoch realized that he had nothing else to do. Perhaps it was intentional, but Janna Logan had left him no further instructions.

10

IAN HAD DIFFICULTY finding a parking spot at Taboo. There was an enormous yellow remote-broadcast TV truck, expensive promotional SUV's from all the big radio stations, and the subtle hint of money everywhere. Must be a big wheel visiting Muskoka, he thought, making another profound and unimportant statement to a breathless public.

Ian smiled. Maybe it was another great plan for the Wharf in Muskoka Bay.

With the crowd congregating in the main building, he thought he'd skip eating. He was hot and tired and his room beckoned, cool and inviting. The window looked out on the full expanse of Lake Muskoka, with Sea Gull Island a wavering mirage in the distance.

There was an envelope propped against the bedside lamp, an invitation from management requesting his presence at a reception and cocktail party to meet "Canada's Greatest Golfer, Mark Watson", from 7 to 9 that evening. In the Winewood Dining Room, it told him, summer casual acceptable.

Ian couldn't figure why he rated an invitation, unless they were inviting everyone who could afford to shell out the money for one of their rooms. Of course, since solving two murders earlier in the year, he'd reluctantly become a recognizable local personality. It was a role he was uncomfortable with, even hated, so he threw the invitation onto the bed.

"That's not for me, I'm not a golfer." He looked at himself in the mirror, but it was his late wife he spoke to, remembering her passion for the sport. "You'd really like to meet a Green Jacket winner, wouldn't you, Caitlin? What the hell, free drinks and a bit of fancy food might be a nice way to spend an hour."

He rubbed his hand over his chin. An excuse to shave and shower would help lift his spirits and besides, Caitlin was telling him to go. This was just the kind of party she loved; short enough to prevent boredom, and just long enough to meet some interesting people. Ian missed her more than he could allow himself to admit.

Mr. and Mrs. Jose de Sa received the same invitation, although they never questioned why. Their wealth, and the two suites of rooms they had booked, warranted at least an invitation to a cocktail party. Xiomara de Sa had actually seen Mark Watson play, winning the Masters in Augusta, and wanted to meet him. Jose insisted she go, hoping she might discreetly find out about Rankin Island. He'd not heard from Orby Lintz in over an hour and his patience, already stretched, was wearing thin.

Under the circumstances, she was glad to get away from her husband. He was involving her in something she was afraid was going to spoil a nice, perfectly comfortable existence. She was beginning to see a side of Jose de Sa she feared. What was his, she learned, was his for keeps. No one could be permitted to take it away, and that meant absolutely no one. He could let the damned gold coins go, for all she cared. He had enough money to last them both a hundred years.

At just one-half inch less than six feet, Xiomara was tall. Her years as a model had taught her to glide, not walk, and her head and neck sat regally on slim, broad shoulders that never wavered as she entered a room. Her waist and hips maintained a single flowing rhythm as long, well-shaped legs floated her into the Winewood Room, just late enough to be fashionable.

By then, Ian had given up on getting near the guest of honour. Television reporters and camera lights, along with a ring of microphone-thrusting radio interviewers, created a formidable barrier around Mark Watson. It was virtually impossible for anyone to get close to the spot he'd taken up by the entrance.

Ian retreated to a window where he could watch the sun on his island. With a plate of shrimp and something unidentifiably delicious on a cracker, he was content to watch the performance of local dignitaries attempting to out-lie each other. Until then, no one had taken any notice of him and it was just the way he wanted it. Until he saw her.

"My God, what a beautiful woman," he said under his breath, startled that he would verbalize such an admission when Caitlin could read his thoughts. Xiomara de Sa's hair formed a shining, ebony halo of ringlets around her tanned face. Dark brows arched above brilliant hazel eyes that, even across a crowded room, Ian couldn't help but notice. Her lips were full and sensual. She wore a yellow silk jacket and long matching dress buttoned from a high oriental collar to a tantalizing slit at the bottom. Her shoes had the highest heels Ian had ever seen. From what he could see of her legs through the crowd, Ian suspected they were perfect.

Ian Murdoch wasn't the only one to notice Xiomara de Sa. Heads turned as she walked to the centre of the room. This woman knew how to make an entrance. It was interesting to watch men gravitate toward her, the women examining every inch of her make-up, clothes and shoes in a futile search for flaws. On his way to refill his scotch and water, their eyes met. Her smile was wide, showing even, white teeth. Since Caitlin's death, Ian couldn't be considered an easy-going person, but when she smiled at him he could feel his own face light up in response. Something had happened and, for the moment, both of them knew it.

A less confidant, more aggressive man would have immediately followed up on the invitation in that smile, but Ian didn't. He couldn't, considering himself a one-woman man and knowing that woman, Caitlin, was gone from his life. He simply returned to take up his place by the window. The west shore of Lake Muskoka cast its long shadow on the water, the sun sliding into the horizon and the void in Murdoch's heart.

Her voice was soft and warm with just the hint of an exotic accent.

"What are you looking at?" Xiomara was standing beside him, lightly scented perfume an intoxicating swirl. Ian couldn't believe it. "You seem lonely."

"Lonely? No, I'm not lonely. I was just looking at the gorgeous view. Sorry if I get melancholy when I see such a magnificent scene." He put out his hand, "Ian Murdoch. And you are?"

"Xiomara de Sa." She pronounced it *See-o-mara*. Her fingers were long, the palm of her hand soft and delicate. She had a strong grip for a woman. "I was watching you and thought you must not be a golfer. You were the only one not trying to push his way nearer the guest of honour. I saw him play the Masters. What's your connection with Mr. Watson?"

"I'm like you, I guess—invited because I'm a guest of the hotel. I was curious, as well." Ian took a deep breath, then forged onward, staring into hazel eyes that were level with his own. Somehow she didn't intimidate him. He felt suddenly comfortable speaking with her. "You certainly added a new dimension to the reception when you walked in. I'd like to add my compliments to a very attractive woman."

The easy chairs opposite the entrance to the Winewood Room were empty. Ian guided Xiomara to two that were facing the windows.

"I've never heard of the name Xiomara. Is it Spanish?"

"Close, but no. It's Greek. My father was Greek and my mother American. I was born in Athens although my mother and I came to America when I was seventeen. My father remained in Greece after they got divorced. I don't know if he's still alive. My husband is Brazilian," she found herself confiding. "He insisted I attend this cocktail party. Hates golf, but he said 'go and meet some of the locals and find out about the area.' It's very beautiful, isn't it?"

"Yes," Ian admitted, although he thought it dimmed somewhat in her presence.

"I see you wear a wedding ring," she commented. "If you don't mind my asking, is your wife here? After all, I've managed to tell you my entire life history in the first two minutes we've known each other."

"I wear a wedding ring because I can't work up the courage to take it off. My wife recently died of cancer."

"And now I know why you look so lonely. You see? I'm a very perceptive person, Mr. Murdoch. This may sound shallow, but I'm sorry about your wife. How long were you married?"

"Fifteen years. No children," he answered in anticipation of her next question. It was what everyone asked. "Let's not dwell on the past. Let me get you another drink and then I'll tell you everything I know about Muskoka. What would you like?"

"Margarita with salt." Xiomara smiled, holding his gaze for a millisecond longer than would customarily be polite.

Walking to the bar, Ian enjoyed a warmth he'd not felt since before Caitlin's illness. He didn't even try to purge his mind of the thoughts that entered it. Attempting to juggle a margarita and double scotch on his way back across the crowded room wasn't easy, however. Especially since Xiomara had attracted several men, the rich and the athletic, and was holding court.

She spotted Ian over an admiring jock's shoulder and skilfully excused herself. Her graceful strides away from the group had all eyes on her shapely body. She linked her arm in Ian's and they walked to the windows overlooking the lake. Sipping her drink, she laughed as she licked the frosted rime from her upper lip.

"Just the way I like it, lots of salt. Now, tell me about your Muskoka."

"Well, the island you see in the foreground is called Lightwood. It was originally purchased from the Crown by a fellow named Harry Mason. He came from a family of piano makers in Toronto and married one of the Gooderhams, the whiskey distillers. This part of Muskoka consists of three main lakes—Muskoka, Rosseau and Joseph. It's some of the most beautiful scenery in Canada."

"Yes, I can see that," she ventured. "No wonder there are so many cottages."

"The original summer visitors, back around the turn of the last century, were the old money of Upper Canada and the northern States. The wealthy of the era came for the entire summer season to exclusive resorts, or built beautiful big seasonal homes. They'd arrive at Gravenhurst in their private train cars with an entourage of gardeners, cooks and nannies for their kids. Then they'd board steamships that would take them to their palatial summer residences."

"It sounds enchanting, yes?"

"Yes, it was a time and lifestyle I envy. Wouldn't it be great to go back to those days when the world had clearly defined principles and respect for the individual? Now, the world is a global village, lines of demarcation in all that matters are fuzzy and sometimes obscure. Just a minute, Xiomara, I'll have to step down from my soapbox. I don't know why I got off on that tangent."

"Because you're a romantic, I suspect." The warmth in her look was all the encouragement he needed, but she asked anyway. "Could you tell me more?"

"These days, it's the nouveau riche, the young lions and the dot-com kids. The Bay Street and Wall Street millionaires are buying up the old cottages and replacing them with gigantic homes. We still have a smattering of stars. It used to be Gable and Garbo, now it's Kurt and Goldie."

"The same thing's happening where I live in Boca Raton, Florida," Xiomara said. "Developers are buying up million-dollar homes around us, then razing them and replacing them with six-million-dollar homes. When the location is right, people will pay any amount of money. It's a cycle that's happening all over the place. We think it's exclusive to our region, but it's happening everywhere I go—Switzerland, Italy, the Riviera and all the major tourist areas."

"You certainly sound well travelled," Ian remarked.

"I've been to these places, even lived in some, and I see the changes. Some good and some bad. Getting back to this lake, my husband has a business acquaintance with a summer place. Would it be on Rankin Island? Can you see that island from here?"

"It's difficult to distinguish, but it's to your left. The west shore of the lake blends into the nearby islands in the dusk, but it's approximately three to four miles as the crow flies." Ian pointed up the lake and she moved closer, her perfume enveloped him. Life was stirring inside. "I'm afraid I'm not much for the stuff they've been serving here. Would you like to join me for something more substantial?"

"Mr. Murdoch, I believe you're a mind reader. I was about to suggest that. I'm so tired of canapés and shrimps that taste like Styrofoam. There are times where I'd give anything for a big, fat, greasy hot dog smothered with mustard and sauerkraut."

"There's another restaurant here, the Wild Fire. Let's give it a try."

They couldn't have asked for a more romantic setting. Rays of dwindling sunlight shot golden shafts across tables of sparkling glass and gleaming silverware. The table they were given was in the farthest corner, by a window.

It had been a long time since Ian had enjoyed a meal with a woman, at least one that wasn't business related. The wine, the food, the ambiance, those flashing hazel eyes and mouth so sensual he couldn't take his eyes away; he was entranced. Conversation went back and forth on mundane subjects but she often returned to Rankin Island. How large is it? How many cottages were there? Ian toyed with the idea of inviting her for a boat ride to see if she could find her husband's friend from Florida, but quickly tossed the idea. His Mickey Mouse old aluminum runabout would do nothing to impress a woman like Xiomara de Sa. Besides, she couldn't remember the friend's name. Ian offered to look him up in the Muskoka Lakes Association's directory. He didn't mention he had access to the 9-1-1 emergency data base that would pinpoint the exact location. He'd long before learned to keep his profession hidden, at least initially. Invariably, people became overly cautious or subdued, as if they were being subjected to interrogation instead of casual conversation. There was always the look that said, "he's a cop—watch what you say." He was adept at recognizing it in faces when people discovered he was a police officer.

Eventually, Xiomara announced that she was tired and wanted to return to her suite. Would Ian care to walk with her? As they made their way down the long corridor, her arm in his, a hundred scenarios flashed through Murdoch's mind. Could this be what he thought? She handed him her card when they arrived at her suite. He slid it into the slot, the green light went on and the lock clicked. She opened the door wide to invite him in.

Hesitating, he thanked her for a lovely evening and turned

away, back to his own room. In the hallway, hearing her door close behind him, he pounded his fist into the palm of his hand. "You stupid bastard," he admonished himself.

In his room the phone was ringing. It was Xiomara. "I've remembered the name of my husband's friend. Peter Crawford."

11

ORBY LINTZ had hooked his camera to the VCR in Jose de Sa's suite. He pushed buttons on the remote and swore, trying to get the video to play. The screen flashed a few times before the picture finally came on. Lintz started to explain.

"All I had to begin with was a photo with 'Rankin Island 02' written on the back. I didn't want to start asking directions from anyone that might be able to identify me down the road, so I got a map of Lake Muskoka and found it myself. I paid cash to rent a boat and went all around the island, videotaping every inch of shoreline. I especially photographed any cottage with a dock sticking out into the lake, like this one." He handed the photograph he had stolen from the late Isobel Crawford to Jose and pointed out the dock.

"I think I've located the cottage where that little bastard is, but I want you to look closely at the tape to confirm it. Have a good look at the screen as I run the tape again and you pick out the place."

A moment later de Sa waved his hand for Lintz to stop the picture. He'd picked the same cottage as Orby. "Have you established that he's there?" he asked in Portuguese.

"Yes, he's there. I went by real slow, pretending that I was fishing, and saw him come out a side door and go around the back of the building. I'm positive it's him but I couldn't take a picture because I was in plain view." Orby disconnected the camera, pulled the film from its casing and placed it in an ashtray by the open window. "He's only sold twenty coins, as far as I can tell, so he must have the rest with him."

As Orby lit a match, preparing to incinerate the film, de Sa stopped him.

"Put that out, you damned fool. It could set off the sprinkler or the smoke alarm. Sometimes, Lintz, I think you're crazy." De Sa's impatience was obvious. "Let me hear your plan. Xiomara is bored stiff, driving me nuts, and I want to get out of this country fast."

"I've rented the boat for two more days," Lintz explained. "You said you wanted to go with me, so I'll pick you up tomorrow morning at the Wharf in Gravenhurst. Dress like we're going fishing. There are no buildings for about three hundred yards on either side of his place. I'll put you ashore where you can't be seen and you work your way back, near his cottage. You can let me know when you're in place with these two-way radios I purchased. I'll pull up to his dock and make like I'm lost, looking for directions or some story. He's never seen me, and before he figures it out we'll have him. I can't wait to see the look on his face when he spots you."

"You can't wait?" the old man exploded. "When I see that smart-assed son of a bitch! If he thinks he can steal my coins, he has another thing coming."

Orby Lintz watched his employer closely. He liked his

cushy job, and the money it paid him, but no one called him crazy. Not even Jose de Sa.

12

WHILE IAN TUCKED into a heart-stopping breakfast, his cell phone buzzed. It was Matt Finnerty. "I tried calling you last night but you had the damned thing shut off again. What were you up to old buddy?" He didn't wait for an answer. "Your father called with a message. His appointment at Princess Margaret Hospital in Toronto is at one-thirty on Friday. He wanted to tell you he'd understand if you can't make it."

"I guess he should," Ian grumbled. "He's never kept a promise in his life. And, as far as what I was up to last night, 'old buddy,' that's no concern of yours. You certainly seem to be taking a keen interest in my personal life. Why don't you let me take a peek into your closet, see if I can find where you've hidden all those skeletons?"

Ian was trying for humour, but Finnerty recognized the tension in his voice.

"Wow, who pissed in your pickles? Listen, Ian, I'm supposed to be your friend. And I'm going to stick my big, red, Irish nose into your personal business when and if I feel a friend needs it. Now, having said that, what have you come up with on the Crawford murder? I understand you questioned the son."

"Yeah. There's something definitely strange about the guy.

J.T. might have mentioned it, but he actually spent a night on my island before this all blew up. Even then he was nervous as a cat. My gut feeling is that he's trying to hide from somebody. We practically had to drag him to the mainland to identify his mother's body." Murdoch took a breath to consider his next request. "I want you to put a trace on him in South Florida, Matt. We found letters from him in his mother's apartment with a Boca Raton address."

"I almost forgot," Matt interrupted. "Your father said a guy answering Peter Crawford's description sold twenty u.s. Liberty gold coins for thirty thousand dollars to the man he works for. A few days later, someone else bought them for the same amount, except in u.s. dollars. Cash, if you can believe it. Do you think this has any bearing on the mother's murder? Sounds a little far-fetched to me."

"You can bet your ass this is relevant, Matt. Can you assign Lou Howard to me exclusively or am I exceeding my authority? After all, Logan is lead officer. I don't like the sound of this, so I want to have Lou keep an eye on him. It'll be difficult because he's holed up on that island, but he'll have to come off to bury his mother in the next two days. We'll spook him if we question him further, but we might get somewhere if we just keep him under surveillance."

"You've got it, friend." Matt agreed.

"Will you tell Logan, or should I?" Murdoch inquired gruffly, giving his superintendent an inkling of what was bothering him.

"Ian, don't get perpendicular on me. I know you're pissed off, but the heat is on with all the recent homicides in

Muskoka. Let's work together to put the lid on this. Janna Logan is a very competent officer and, on top of that, a good, decent person. You have the balls, Ian. Work with her for the good of the force."

"Okay, Matt. I'll be in Toronto for J.T.'s appointment on Friday," he continued. "J.T. has actually seen Crawford, so his ID should be good, but I want to talk to his boss about the guy who purchased the coins. I think the kid's in deep shit."

Punching "end" on his cell, Ian was crossing the lobby when he heard Xiomara's softly accented voice, tinged with a note of sarcasm.

"And how did you sleep last night, Ian?" She was impeccably dressed in a white suit with a very short, tight skirt and high heels that combined to show lots of leg. The short jacket had long sleeves and a rounded boat-neck, her breasts filling it out enough to emphasize a slim waist. A delicate silver chain hung just below the neckline, the ensemble complemented by a loosely tied pink scarf. Ian was speechless.

"What are you up to today, Mr. Murdoch?" Still irony in her voice.

Ian suspected she might be smarting from the way he'd retreated from her earlier invitation. She didn't seem the type of woman to take rejection lightly, especially in the uncivilized boonies of Canada. He wanted to make amends. He couldn't resist her.

"Xiomara. I have some business this morning, but I was about to call and invite you to lunch. Maybe I could show you a little of the area. Interested?"

"Well, my husband's going fishing this morning and he'll be

gone all day. I'd be pleased to see the sights and have lunch with you. Can I meet you in the lobby at noon? Is that okay?" Her voice had reverted to the sweetness of maple syrup.

"Certainly. Noon it is."

Ian watched her glide away, every eye in the lobby upon her. He shook his head. "How could you be so stupid?" he muttered to himself.

He made arrangements to join Lou Howard at the Bracebridge crime scene. Fingerprints lifted from the kitchen area had all been identified. They belonged to either the deceased or her live-in boyfriend. That left only partial thumb and forefinger prints on an empty picture frame in the bedroom. Thinking of Crawford's Florida connection, Ian asked Lou to run them by the FBI stateside.

"Logan's already beat you to it," Lou confessed. "We should have some results in the next day or two."

Neighbours on either side and above had been questioned. So far, everyone seen entering or leaving the apartment had been identified and accounted for.

"God, Lou," Ian bitched. "Another dead end. Have we got anything that even remotely looks like a lead?"

"This Norm Stokes guy, the significant other, is ex-army. He brags around the transport depot that he was in the old Airborne Regiment and knows a hundred ways to kill a man with his bare hands. He's clean so far, but just to double check we're pulling the company's print-out of his movements from the day prior to the day after Isobel Crawford's murder."

"It would be interesting to see if there's any possibility he could've parked his rig and got back here." Both men looked up in surprise to realize that Janna Logan had silently entered the room.

"There's no forced entry," Lou said, "so we're assuming she let her assailant in. Truckers are notorious for parking their rigs and doubling back home to catch the old lady with the Polish boarder."

Ian looked at Lou, perplexed.

"An old joke, Ian. You know the one? Teacher asks where the Polish border is and the kid says 'Home in bed with my mother.' What's with you, Ian? You're a million miles away."

"It would help if it was a better joke," Logan deadpanned.

"Sorry, Lou, I've got an appointment in Gravenhurst this afternoon. I was thinking about that." Ian stared into the middle distance for a moment. "Okay, let's recap what we've got. First, we think that Peter Crawford sold thirty thousand dollars worth of gold coins in Toronto last week. An unidentified man purchased them shortly after using u.s. hundred-dollar bills and, very shortly after that, Crawford's mother is murdered. There's something strange about this, and it can't be coincidental."

"So, let's get those partial fingerprints back from the FBI pronto," Logan interrupted. "Meanwhile, we figure a way to keep this kid under surveillance. If he isn't the killer, he may have hired someone or know who it was. Also, I'll check to see if she had insurance and if the contents of the apartment are worth anything."

"His alibi is iron clad right now," Ian mused. "We have to find a way to beat it. I have my cell on, you can get me any time."

He directed his comment to Lou, knowing full well that he hadn't given his number to Logan.

Ian tried not to think of Caitlin, but she wouldn't leave his mind as he drove south on Highway 11 to Gravenhurst. He wondered if she thought him a fool. Stopping at the small beach parking lot near the mouth of the Hoc Roc, he hid the emergency flashing light, and any police paraphernalia that wasn't screwed down, before travelling the last few hundred yards. Pulling to a stop in front of Taboo's lobby he could see Xiomara waving from inside. She hadn't changed her dress, but she'd added a pair of designer sunglasses. Slipping into the seat beside him, her long, graceful legs were exposed well above the knee. Ian gave them a double take, not very subtly, and she laughed. Surprisingly, she leaned over and kissed him on the cheek.

They drove along the bay at Gravenhurst. The *Wenonah II* could be seen beyond the construction, loading passengers for an afternoon cruise. The *Segwun*, which he explained was the country's oldest operational steamship, was already out for the day. He didn't bother to tell her about his recent investigation involving the historic old ship, but he was hoping they'd spot it somewhere around the lake as they drove. At the Wharf Project, preparations were well under way on the site for new restaurants, shops and hotels, and the bay area, he lamented, would be a mess for at least the next year. Xiomara, he noticed, wasn't very interested in the best-laid plans of mice, men or Muskoka Bay dreamers.

At Bala, however, she was very interested in The Kee, the old Dunn's Pavilion, where the Duke and Count Basie had played with their bands. In times past, the Dorsey Brothers had been regulars every summer. Xiomara was a swing era enthusiast.

"I love to dance," she told him. "I think I'm quite good." Ian could imagine that she was. She admitted having CD's of all the old swing orchestras.

They drove over the bridge by the little stone church, now an antique shop, and parked at the top of the hill. Hand in hand they crossed the road to see the Moon River thundering out of Lake Muskoka, over timeworn Precambrian rock toward Georgian Bay. Plumes of white water leapt in the air, then swirled and eddied at the bottom before winding silently through the canyon of trees beyond.

Leaning over the rail, Ian could see that Xiomara was visibly nervous, a result of the noise and tumbling water below. He self-consciously put his arm around her waist and she leaned her head on his shoulder. A strange feeling came over him; he began feeling sorry for Xiomara. She had everything, a graceful aura, a body that wouldn't quit and a beautiful face, and yet Ian sensed that she too was lonely. Experience had honed his sense of perception to such a degree that he was sensitive to a person's inner feelings.

He wondered if, like so many that trade love and family for wealth and security, perhaps Xiomara found it unfulfilling. Had she woken one day and asked herself if it was worth it? As Peggy Lee sang, "Is that all there is?" Ian knew the feeling. Caitlin couldn't have children and, although they had talked about adopting, she got sick and that was that. Even if Ian hadn't seen Xiomara's husband, he knew instinctively that she'd never be any more than another of his possessions. How long ago had she begun to realize it? Otherwise, why

would she have gravitated to a gnarled old gimp of a cop.
They drove to Port Carling in silence, past the exits for
Acton Island, Mortimer's Point and Butterfly Lake. Ian parked
at the locks and, looking down the Indian River, was pleased
to see the RMS *Segwun*. The old girl was steaming silently
for the open lock that would raise her to the level of Lake
Rosseau. It was a stroke of luck. Xiomara would get to see
the beautiful old lady while she slipped ever so slowly past,
the telegraph clanging "Stop Engines," and the gate closing
behind her. They stood so close they could distinguish the
pungent smell of burning coal from the distinct, almost sweet
odour of lubricating oil around the engines. Periodic hisses
of steam punctuated conversation and sent waves of excitement through the small crowd along both the docks and the
decks of the ship. Everyone was caught up in the magic of
the moment, listening to the lap of water as the level rose,
then watching the wooden ship glide majestically through.
There was something seemingly effortless about the historic
ship's passage into the upper lake. It was a spectacle that had
lost none of its charm despite a century of repetition.

It was well past lunchtime and they were both hungry. Ian
decided Windermere would be a gorgeous setting for lunch,
even if it meant waiting even longer while they made the scenic drive through Brackenrig. They ate under gnarled old
maples, on a patio overlooking the lake. Ian explained how
the Windermere House had burned and was rebuilt as close
to the original style as modern safety requirements would
allow. Emptying the last of their white wine, they walked to
the wooden Muskoka chairs peculiar to the region. On the
lawn, facing the lake, Ian couldn't help himself. He kissed her.

Far from shying away, Xiomara melted against him. They sat, holding hands.

"Close your eyes," Ian instructed her. "Imagine a hundred years ago, sitting right here, watching the *Segwun* coming in to dock. Men in white suits and straw skimmers, women with long skirts, puff-sleeved blouses and wide-brimmed hats with fringed parasols. Children, perhaps, with their short pants and little beanies. All coming for the summer at Windermere House in Muskoka."

The hypnotic moment was too good to last. It was shattered by the buzz of Ian's cell phone.

"Murdoch," he said, forcing a smile of apology for Xiomara's benefit. "Jesus, no. I'm at Windermere right now, Lou. Pick me up at the Wharf in Gravenhurst in about an hour, depending on traffic. Get Logan on the blower and have her meet us there."

Xiomara shot him a look of equal parts concern and curiosity as he flipped his phone closed.

"I'm sorry, Xiomara. I have to take you back to Taboo."

"Is something the matter?"

"I'm a police officer," Ian confessed with gravity. "It's nothing personal, but a man we've had under surveillance has had his cottage burnt to the ground. We suspect he was in it."

"That's terrible," she whispered in alarm. "Of course we have to go."

Ian hesitated for a second, then dropped his bad news.

"His name is Peter Crawford."

"Oh, my God. That's my husband's friend." The blood drained from her face as she blurted the words.

Rushing to the car, Ian retrieved the emergency light from

the trunk and attached it to the dash. As they turned out of the parking lot he activated the flasher. He didn't slow again until they reached Bracebridge twenty-five minutes later. From there, the drive to Taboo was made in complete silence. At the resort, Ian watched as she threw long legs out of the car and ran to the hotel. They didn't bother with good-byes. When he'd seen her safely inside, he finally voiced his concern.

"God, Xiomara, I hope you're not involved in this fiasco."

13

JANNA WAS ALREADY AT THE BOAT. The young OPP marine officer had moored at the end of a floating dock and directed Ian to park by the Pavilion. With construction of the Wharf Project under way, it was the only space available.

"Where's Sergeant Howard?" Ian inquired.

"That's what I have to tell you, sir. A fishing boat with two people on board ran smack into Twin Rocks at full throttle, just east of your island. One man's badly hurt, but the other's not as bad. Sergeant Howard got a 9-1-1 call patched through from a Mr. Flannigan who saw the whole thing from his cottage on the mainland."

"It was bound to happen sooner or later," Ian said. He knew the spot well and wondered how tourists, unfamiliar with the lake, had managed to miss the Twins for so many years. "I just wish it hadn't happened now."

"He said the boat was going like hell," the young uniform continued. "Either the driver didn't know how to trim the motor or the bow was way up in the air. Anyway, the driver slammed right into them. The boat went up in the air, the driver went flying over the bow and the passenger, an older man, hit the dashboard. Sounds like he stove in his chest pretty seriously. He's in bad shape. Paramedics took both of them to hospital in Bracebridge and Sergeant Howard's at the scene now."

"When did all this happen?" Logan yelled over the noise of the motor as they accelerated out of Muskoka Bay.

"Just after the Sergeant called in the fire. He went to the scene to co-ordinate the search in case there were more passengers. The guy that was hurt least wasn't talking so we can't be sure until we've searched. In fact, they had a hell of a time just convincing him to go to hospital. He wanted to stay with the boat. Don't know why, the motor's torn right off and the hull is smashed to bits. All the fishing tackle and junk in the boat went straight into the drink."

They detoured around the point near Flannigan's so Ian could see the accident scene at Twin Rocks. Large pieces of fibreglass hull were hung up on the rocks, the motor twisting away at ninety degrees. A few curious boaters circled the wreckage and the detachment's only other police boat was trying to keep them at a distance. Howard was nowhere in sight. Feeling like a rubber-necker, Ian nodded to his young skipper and they proceeded on to Peter Crawford's burntout cottage.

"Any word on the boater's identity?" Logan asked, making casual conversation.

"Yes, Ma'am," the constable replied. "Some old guy from the States. De Sa, I think. Probably a cottager."

Murdoch's reaction startled the younger officer. He pushed forward on the throttle, steering toward the light column of smoke visible against the approaching tree line.

At Rankin Island, four boats were already tied to Crawford's small dock. They moored alongside one and had to scramble to the landing. White smoke rose in patches from the pile of black rubble. As they reached solid ground, Ian was surprised to see Lou Howard there, out of uniform, which was just as well. He was covered in dirt and soot that ran in rivulets of sweat. Howard took Ian aside before they reached the remains of the cottage.

"I borrowed a boat from Albert Cowan and parked her on the east shore, opposite Crawford's cottage. I thought it would be the best way to keep the poor bastard under surveillance. Had a hell of a time tying up, it was so shallow that boat wakes made the propeller bump the rocks. If it hadn't taken me so long, I might have been here to pull him out." Lou took a deep lungful of air before continuing.

"When I did get here, the place was totally engulfed. The wood was so old and dry it went up like paper. I called Albert on my cell and he came with his pumper boat, but all he could do was keep the fire from spreading. By the time the fire department arrived it was all over. Those other boats at the dock are just people who saw the fire and came to help. The Fire Marshal is on his way from Gravenhurst now."

"Are you sure Crawford was in the cottage?" Logan asked, shielding her hair and face as they got too close to the smoking ruins. The heat quickly drove them back a few feet.

"No, I'm not positive. I couldn't get that close, but I could see inside the cottage through one window. There was no movement of any kind and he hadn't left the property. You know, Ian, this place went up so fast there must have been some kind of accelerant."

"Are you even sure there was anyone inside?" Ian tried to get closer.

"You remember, Ian, once you smell burning flesh, you never forget the stench. I think that lump you can see near the doorway is a body." Howard pointed to a rise in the pile of smouldering ash.

"If so, maybe that's the murder in Bracebridge solved for us," Logan speculated.

Ian's cell phone buzzed. It was his father. He walked away from the group of onlookers to take the call but Logan could still make out his end of the conversation.

"What's up, J.T.? Sell how many? All Liberty and Maple Leaf coins, eh? Holy shit, how much money is that? And you're sure it was Peter Crawford—when?"

Logan wondered at the coincidence of the call.

"Thanks, Dad. I'm sorry, but it's starting to look like I won't be able to get to Toronto on Friday after all. And Dad, you'd better tell your boss there's a chance the deal won't go through. But if Peter Crawford does show up, I need to know immediately. Okay, you take care of yourself, too."

Ian called Lou and Janna over.

"That was my Dad," he informed them. "J.T. works for a coin dealer in Toronto and it turns out they had a call from Peter Crawford this morning. He was inquiring about selling $350,000 worth of gold coins. The deal's supposed to go down tomorrow. Apparently he was about to take off on a trip."

"I guess that rules out suicide," Logan offered.

The Fire Marshal had arrived and was cautiously walking the ruins, photographing every step of the way. He had his own people pulling debris away from the front door. It was definitely a body, face down in the superheated ash. One arm was obviously turned under the torso, the other extended and badly burned, almost beyond recognition. The backs of what Murdoch assumed were legs seemed charred through to the bone.

Ian took his turn photographing every angle of the body and surrounding area before Logan allowed paramedics to put it into a body bag. She instructed them on its delivery to Bracebridge and watched as they carried the blackened, unrecognizable corpse away.

"Well, what do you think, Lou? Is it Crawford?"

"Hard to tell at this point."

"You'd better make arrangements to have the coin dealership in Toronto watched tomorrow." Logan wiped sweat and soot from her brow. "If Crawford does show up, he may have another murder to answer for."

"And if he doesn't show?" asked Lou.

"Then I think we know who our body is." Ian considered the irony of Crawford lying next to his mother in the mortuary. If the son had been planning to take off with a small fortune, it wasn't much of a trip.

The Fire Marshal walked over to speak to Ian and Lou. Reluctantly Murdoch asked him to include Logan in the conversation.

"We've got a lot more work to do on this site and I won't be able to give you a report for a few days. God only knows if this was arson or not, although I'd guess it was. I've seen a lot of fires, but this one sure as hell wiped this place out in a hurry. It has all the earmarks of an accelerant, but there's no hard evidence so far. We've further tests to do and they'll tell us something. I'll call my findings into you before sending the official report."

"Address them to me at Orillia," Logan requested.

14

XIOMARA KEPT CALLING HER HUSBAND, utilizing the speed dial on her cell phone. When there was still no answer after several attempts, she tried Orby Lintz as a last resort. No answer from him, either. She was frantic.

"Why did we come here?" She asked herself again and again, pacing the floor. Lintz made her nervous and, coupled with the recent changes she'd noticed in her husband's behaviour, she had a sick feeling in the pit of her stomach. "God, I hope it's nothing to do with that fire. What a fool I was to mention Peter Crawford's name to Ian. Oh God, Jose, I didn't know he was a cop. I just didn't know!"

Her self-recrimination was interrupted by a polite knock at the door. It was the hotel manager.

"Mrs. de Sa," he began with obvious distress. "I'm sorry to tell you that your husband has been in an accident. He's in South Muskoka Hospital in Bracebridge." Xiomara was struck dumb by the news, but the manager was both sympathetic and efficient. "I've a car waiting and we'll take you there immediately."

"Accident? Was it a car accident? How serious—was anyone else hurt?" The questions flooded Xiomara's mind as the car raced up the back road to Bracebridge. She was terrified of the answer to the one question she couldn't possibly ask. "Had it been a fire?"

The manager dropped her at the hospital's Emergency entrance, offering to wait at the admissions desk in the event she needed him. He arranged for a kindly volunteer to deliver Xiomara to an office adjacent to the Emergency Trauma Centre. Xiomara watched the elderly volunteer approach a doctor and speak quietly with him. Throwing his latex gloves in a waste bucket, the doctor shrugged his shoulders and walked to the office where Xiomara sat ashen-faced.

"Mrs. de Sa, I'm Dr. O'Grady. I'm very sorry, but your husband's injuries were severe. We tried everything to revive him, but his heart had been punctured." He looked closely at Xiomara and took note of her lack of understanding. Holding her hand, he sat next to her. "Has it been explained that he was a passenger in a boat that struck a group of rocks? No, I didn't think so. I'm sorry, but it appears as if your husband was thrown into the dashboard of the boat on impact, probably the cause of his broken ribs. One of the ribs punctured the right ventricle of Mr. de Sa's heart. This was the cause of his death."

Xiomara took a deep breath and closed her eyes against the tears. Even in grief, O'Grady realized, this is a beautiful woman. She certainly wouldn't be allowed to grieve alone for long.

"Is there anyone we can call? Anyone who can be with you?"

Nothing in her life had prepared her for this. First there was relief at the realization Jose had not suffered from burns, removing the worry of his involvement with the fire. And then came the absolute and utter shock of complete loss. Jose de Sa, if not a loving husband, had been her benefactor and companion, her friend. She didn't know what emotion followed, wasn't aware that she had put her face in her hands and begun to sob. O'Grady, the big Irish doctor, well schooled in tragedy, gently placed an arm around her. She buried her face in his shoulder, convulsing in waves of tears.

"Can I get you a drink? Coffee or soda? I might even find a drink of medicinal brandy if you'd like." She reached for a box of tissues on the desk and he at least managed to provide that for her. Gradually, Xiomara began to regain some control.

"You said my husband was a passenger. What happened to the other person?"

"Mr. Lintz," O'Grady smiled thinly, pleased at last to provide some good news. "He's in emergency. He has a badly bruised shoulder, three cracked ribs and other minor abrasions. Other than that, he's in reasonably good shape. Apparently he flew over the bow when the boat hit the rocks, landing in the water. That probably saved his life. He's been constantly asking to see you, by the way. A very impatient man, our Mr. Lintz. If you feel up to it, I can have the nurse bring him here."

"Yes, of course. I want to know what happened. They were just going fishing this morning ..." She left her doubts unspoken, brushing her hand over her tear-streaked make-up.

Orby Lintz walked with some difficulty, obviously in pain

but refusing to use a wheelchair. He entered the office and perched himself on O'Grady's desk. Xiomara asked the doctor if they could have a moment's privacy.

When they were alone, Lintz was first to speak.

"I never saw the goddamn rocks before we smashed into them. One minute Jose was insisting I look at his prize catch, and the next I was over the windshield. He was sitting down and must've struck the front cockpit. Everything in the boat went into the water, including me." He leaned over and whispered in Xiomara's ear. "The gold coins were in a plastic fishing tackle box. They're at the bottom of the lake near that bunch of rocks."

"To hell with the coins." It was her turn to whisper. "You two burned down that Crawford's cabin and he was in it. That makes you both murderers, and you're the only one left."

"Lookit, bitch, there's no 'to hell with the coins.' There's a million in gold at the bottom of that lake and I'm going to get it." Lintz gave her a stare intended to intimidate. "And don't give me that sanctimonious shit about murder. You knew why we came here. Did you think that young fucker was going to give up a million bucks without a fight? He stole those coins from your husband, but maybe that slipped your mind. Where the hell did you think the money came from for you to flaunt your pretty ass around Boca Raton? Did you think Jose de Sa was selling encyclopedias?"

He waited for a response, then pushed closer with the knowledge that she had been sufficiently subdued.

"No, you're not that stupid," he hissed. "You're going to do exactly as I tell you. You go back to your hotel, keep your mouth shut and talk to no one. There'll have to be an inquest where I'll take all the blame for the accident. I was unfamiliar with the rocks and I was driving a boat that I wasn't used to, it's as simple as that. There's no way they can hold me responsible for Jose's death. And there's no way the cops will connect us with that fire. Understand?"

A cold hand gripped Xiomara's heart as she thought of Ian Murdoch. She'd always known Orby Lintz had a dark side and, looking into his cold grey eyes, she was frightened. He'd stop at nothing to get the gold now that both Jose and Peter Crawford were dead.

"I'll go back to my hotel as soon as they discharge me from the hospital," Lintz continued. "The police'll want me to stay in town until the inquest and that'll give me time to work out a plan. Make no mistake, I'm going to get them. That'll be my kiss off, so when this is over you'll never see me again. Unless, of course, you want to." The smile he flashed filled her with revulsion.

"Give me your cell phone," he demanded. "Mine went into the drink. I know your number at the hotel if I have to get in touch with you. Remember, all you know is that your husband and I went fishing before the accident."

Without further explanation, he hobbled from the room. Xiomara took some satisfaction in watching him walk with great difficulty. A moment later, Dr. O'Grady returned with a glass and a can of soda.

"I brought you a brandy," he smiled. "The soda's just a disguise. I'm afraid there's another person who needs to speak with you first. I wouldn't bother you, but it seems urgent.

He's an Ontario Provincial Police officer, name of Ian Murdoch. A little moody, but he's a decent guy if you feel up to talking to him."

15

HIS BRIEF SOJOURN WITH XIOMARA had affected Ian Murdoch more than he cared to admit. When he turned from Highway 11 onto Taylor Road, en route to South Muskoka Hospital in Bracebridge, he'd already decided to question Xiomara first.

When he found her in O'Grady's office, she looked devastated. Her hair was untidy, reddened eyes with mascara smudging the lower lids showing that she'd been crying. Ian had to bring himself up short. Empathy, not sympathy, he reminded himself. He was sure there was a link between her husband's accident and the fire at Rankin Island. More important, he was sure that she knew what that link really was. Still, he took both of her hands and looked deeply into her swollen eyes as she stood to meet him.

"I'm so sorry, Xiomara. I went to the accident scene and the boat was a total wreck. I could see that your husband didn't have a chance of surviving the crash. If there's anything you need help with, I'm at your disposal." Her hands were trembling. Murdoch guided her back to the chair.

"Oh, Ian, I don't know what to do. I've no knowledge of my husband's business affairs. I only came up here to get away from the summer heat in Florida and I don't even know why he came here. As I told you at lunch, he and Orby Lintz, a business acquaintance, were going fishing this morning."

Ian listened carefully, wondering if she was being spontaneous or deliberately drawing a line in the sand.

"They go fishing in Florida a lot," she lied, working up to her next question. "Will you come with me to the funeral director? I'll have to make arrangements to fly Jose to Florida for cremation."

"Certainly I'll go with you, but we can't release him until the Coroner's performed an autopsy."

"An autopsy? I thought that was only required if a crime was committed." Xiomara was getting very nervous. "I thought there'd just be an inquest or something."

"An autopsy is done in Ontario whenever there's any accident involving a death. It's only routine in your husband's case." Ian could stretch the truth to suit his purposes as easily as the next person. "Your husband will be released to you within the next few days, I'm sure. And yes, there'll also be an inquest into his death. I don't think it'll be necessary for you to attend. Again, this is strictly routine. It's obvious that Mr. Lintz wasn't familiar with the shoals in the lake. A witness on shore saw the whole thing. He said the bow of the boat was high out of the water, obscuring Lintz's vision. He'll be called to testify because he was driving the boat, and the formality of the inquest must be adhered to. I'm sure the judge will find him blameless and your husband's death will be declared accidental."

Xiomara seemed relieved, quickly regaining her composure.

"Would you please take me back to the hotel?" she asked. "Suddenly I'm very tired."

"Certainly."

"And, Ian," she pressed his hands. "Could you have dinner with me tonight? I don't want to be alone."

"I'd be happy to. In fact, I sent the manager back to Taboo when I arrived, so it looks as if I'm your ride, anyway. However, I'll need to ask you to wait a few minutes. I just have to ask your husband's friend a few questions before I go."

Orby Lintz was impatiently waiting on a gurney in a curtained cubical of the emergency room.

"Ian Murdoch, Mr. Lintz. I'm an Inspector with the Ontario Provincial Police. I can see you're pretty banged up, so I'll make this brief."

"Go ahead," Lintz grunted. "I'm not going anywhere."

"Were you familiar with the operation of trimming the motor on a boat to run it on even keel at a fast speed?" Ian had decided to approach the accident obliquely.

"I tried to adjust the angle of the boat, but it didn't seem to cooperate," Lintz said as Ian took notes.

"How about an estimate of your speed when you hit the rocks? In either miles or kilometres per hour, if you'd like."

"I couldn't say about kilometres, but I'd estimate eighteen to twenty-five miles per hour. Not overly fast, really." Lintz wasn't volunteering anything beyond the questions Ian asked.

"I understand you were fishing with the deceased. Have you been on Lake Muskoka before?"

"Yeah, we were fishing but, no, this is my first trip here."

"You understand that the inquest won't be for a few days

and you'll have to attend? It'll be here in Bracebridge and you'll be contacted. Where can I reach you if I have further questions, Mr. Lintz?"

"I've a room in town. I've already given that information to the other cops."

"Oh, just one more question," Ian asked as he prepared to leave. "Did you and Jose de Sa go fishing often?"

"Never. This is the first time." Lintz knew immediately this wasn't a dumb question from a rube cop.

Ian had seen Lintz's type a hundred times before. He was a cool, calculating son of a bitch. His eyes gave him away. This bastard could kill without compunction, Murdoch thought, deciding to let Lintz think he was dealing with just another country bumpkin.

Ian could see Xiomara watching from the office as walked back to her. On his way, the doctor interrupted his passage.

"I was attending at the preparation for the autopsy on your burn victim and thought you might want our preliminary findings, Inspector. Young male, of course, but his neck was broken. Whatever killed him, it wasn't the fire." O'Grady watched for Ian's reaction and saw no surprise. "The left hand didn't sustain any burns, I understand, because it was protected under the body. It's interesting to note that the bones at the tips of three fingers had been crushed. The autopsy will tell us more, of course. It'll be at eight, tomorrow morning. In the meanwhile, we've X-rayed and sent the dental information out to local dentists to see if any can identify him."

"Thank you." Ian shook O'Grady's hand. "You're sure he was dead before the fire?"

"Not enough smoke in the lungs to have asphyxiated him,

I'm afraid. I hope this isn't going to make your job a lot harder."

"It's never easy. Fortunately, it isn't really my job. Can I ask you to provide a written report for Detective Sergeant Janna Logan?"

O'Grady observed Ian as he started to leave. "It's nice to see you again, Inspector. You can hardly notice any difference in your walk."

Ian went immediately to Xiomara who appeared more nervous by the minute. It was exactly the way he wanted her. As he'd suspected, there were now two murders: Isobel and Peter Crawford. He knew he was jumping to conclusions, assuming that the burned body was Peter's, but the crushed fingertips on both were more than coincidental. He'd never get Orby Lintz to admit to anything, he was too cute by far, but Lintz's arrival in the area and the death of Jose de Sa had to be connected. The image of gold coins kept popping into his brain.

Xiomara was the key.

The drive back to Taboo was strained. Xiomara sat, gorgeous legs showing almost up to her hips, folding and unfolding her hands in worry. Two or three times, sobs racked her body as she stared unseeing out the window. As she rushed through the lobby to her room, her only words to Ian were, "Don't leave me alone tonight, please."

From his own room, Ian immediately called Lou Howard.

"Lou, Orby Lintz has been patched up at the hospital and will be going to his hotel as soon as he's released. Don't let that mother out of your sight. He's our number one suspect in both Peter Crawford's and his mother's murder. Be very careful, Lou, this Lintz is slippery and likely dangerous. What did you hear on the use of an accelerant at the fire scene?"

"Nothing yet." Lou didn't have a chance to continue, let alone question Ian's assumption that it was Crawford's body that had been found.

"Pick me up early tomorrow morning," Murdoch forged on. "Say five o'clock at Muskoka Wharf. You and I are going over that fire scene with a fine-toothed comb. Those two people were murdered for a reason, Lou, and my gut feeling is that Crawford's gold coins are at the heart of it all."

"Five o'clock? Don't you ever sleep?" Lou was steaming.

"Autopsy's at eight. By the time we reach the island we should have enough light to work by."

16

WHAT TO WEAR to a beautiful woman's room for dinner? It wasn't a situation Ian was overly familiar with. Especially since the woman in question was in a distraught state and he still wanted to carefully interrogate her. She knew the link, he was sure, between the dead mother, the fire, and the charred corpse. Ian had trained himself to detach emotions from his investigations, but since Caitlin's death it was becoming harder each day. Something was different. First, the loss of his wife, then the loss of a young officer he'd become fond of. And now? He'd become fond of Xiomara, as well, but was it going beyond caring, or had it blossomed into desire? She was a gorgeous woman, her beauty something both fascinating and familiar, and she stirred emotions he thought were dead. Murdoch, brutally honest with himself, admitted that he wanted her.

After a shower, shave and careful dressing in slacks, Hawaiian shirt and loafers, Ian was as ready as he would ever be.

Xiomara answered her door wrapped in a Taboo bathrobe. Her hair was towelled but not untidy and her make-up had been repaired. It was still apparent she'd been crying. The whites of those large, hazel eyes were streaked with spider veins of red. She was barefoot.

"Oh, Ian, I've been going crazy." She led him into her spacious suite and they settled near the windows. "I don't know what to do. Jose never let me do the banking, household expenses, or anything to do with his business. He kept it all to himself. I haven't even made out a cheque since we were married. Jose was a very secretive man. I don't think even Orby Lintz knows half the business my husband was involved in."

This was the opening Ian needed.

"What business, that you know of, was your husband involved with?"

"I know he was involved in financing shopping centres and office buildings in Brazil, Portugal and Spain. People came to our home at Boca, architects and owners, to discuss their buildings with him at dinner. The dinners were where I'd find out about my husband's public business. But there were many other men that visited our home in Royal Palm that I was never introduced to. A lot of meetings behind closed doors." For a moment, Xiomara was lost in thought.

"My husband has a lawyer in Boca Raton. I've met him many times over dinner, as well. I called him and he's flying up here later tomorrow. Lintz called him before I did, though." Murdoch thought he noticed a tone of disgust each · time she mentioned Orby Lintz by name. "He's picking him up at Muskoka Airport. I don't know if I'm being paranoid, but I get the feeling I'm somehow being shut out. I don't know if my husband had a will, or where to find it if he had. I'm sure he must have, but I'm so confused." She sat on the over-stuffed couch, folding and unfolding her hands.

"I'm very sorry, Xiomara, I can't help when it comes to Florida law." Ian sat beside her. "If you feel you're being side-tracked, I think your best solution would be to get your own lawyer. You must have a friend who could steer you to a good estate lawyer. I understand Boca Raton is full of them." Ian hesitated, simply wanting to hold her. His emotions were at war with his professional self. Was it sympathy, empathy or just plain desire? It didn't seem to matter any longer.

"I'll get the Death Certificate for you tomorrow. You can fax it to the lawyer from the hotel."

"Oh, you beautiful man. You've given me a great idea." She turned and looked Ian in the eyes, cupping his face to kiss him quickly and fully on the mouth. "My best girlfriend's husband is a lawyer for a big firm. They handle probates, trusts and all that stuff. I'll call first thing in the morning."

Her response surprised even Xiomara, leaving Murdoch breathless and in a state of shock. For a moment they could do nothing more than look at each other. Xiomara finally broke the awkwardness of the moment.

"You know Ian, it's like a huge weight has been lifted. I'm hungry. What would you like to eat?"

"Easy on the compliments. I'm a neophyte when it comes

to estate law in Florida, but I'm hungry, too. Would you like to dress first, or just call room service?" He welcomed the change of subject, and the abrupt change in her mood. Another kiss like that, however, and he knew he was done for.

Opening the leather-bound listing of hotel amenities, she exclaimed, "You can have almost anything they serve in the dining rooms. How about prime rib, baked potato and vegetable medallions? Now to find the wine list." She thumbed through the pages and, in disgust, said, "Two bottles of Chateauneuf du Pape is about the best we can do. That's a decent French red, at least."

Xiomara dialled room service and Ian marvelled at how efficiently she ordered. There was no doubt that she was used to hotel life. A connoisseur he was not. He'd never heard of Chateau-whatsit du Pape. Merlot was what he'd always ordered and the extent of his knowledge. He felt slightly intimidated by her sophistication. He had to get her back on track.

"Do you think Lintz was being helpful, or does he have an agenda of his own?" Ian didn't even bother to ease into the subject. "I find it strange that he'd call your husband's lawyer and not tell you he'd done that. Would picking him up at the airport perhaps have something to do with the business your husband and Lintz were in Muskoka for?" He knew what her answer would be. She'd claim absolutely no knowledge of her husband's affairs. It was the expression on her face that Ian was watching for. The eyes were a dead giveaway.

There was a knock at the door and a white-coated waiter wheeled in a cart. The aroma of food filled the room.

"Oh, man, am I hungry." Ian said, and smiled at the realization they had spoken in unison. It was the kind of thing that he and Caitlin would do, based on long years of familiarity. The table by the window was soon set with endless cutlery and wine glasses. When the waiter uncovered enormous plates of prime rib, the arrangement looked perfect. As he opened the first bottle of wine and presented the cork, Ian couldn't believe the condition of the bottle. It looked like it had survived a fire, aged and dusty. The waiter left the cork.

Xiomara signed the bill, adding a gratuity that made the waiter all but fall on his knees. His thanks kept up until he was out the door.

Their view of the setting sun was partially obscured by a large jack pine. Golden rays cast long shadows on the wine glasses, cutlery reflecting the last light of an emotional and eventful day for them both. Xiomara's face was radiant in the dying glow of light. In spite of the interruption and those beautiful eyes, Murdoch instinctively knew that Xiomara would have lied in response to his questions. The sun's golden glow cast a spell of intimacy over them both and honesty was lost in the moment.

She had a few seconds to compose herself, taking a large sip of wine. Her liquid eyes darkened as she watched Ian over the rim of her glass. She knew he'd continue to ask probing questions. She didn't care. This man was here with her now. She knew for certain that he wanted her just as much as she needed him.

"Please, Ian, call me Mara. Xiomara is so formal." She picked at the last of her meal. "I was surprised at how hungry I was."

She'd drunk most of the first bottle of wine and was well into the second. Ian's own capacity was limited to one glass, his second still half-full. Mara was obviously starting to feel her alcohol, and it showed in her loss of inhibitions.

"When I lived in Greece, I think I was about seventeen, I had an affair with a married man. He was the love of my life but, when my mother found out, she was furious. Not only at me. The man was a business partner of my father's. This was the last straw for my parent's marriage, it had been in the toilet for years. The macho society of Greece had proven too much for her. My mother packed up and we moved back to New York—alone."

Talk continued until the end of the second bottle. Their conversation had become a ritual, a dance that could conclude in making love. Love was not an honest word.

With the death of her husband, Mara would have to face a future full of questions. Her comfy life with Jose de Sa was gone forever, temporarily replaced by desire for a man to wrap his arms around her. Ian's own desire had possessed him completely. For a year before Caitlin's death there had been no sex in his life, only compassion. His need for a woman was overwhelming. Could he deny it? He closed his eyes and pondered the question.

It was only when he opened his eyes that he realized Mara had turned off the lights. He could hear her softly breathing, a sound like a cat purring.

Later, his room cool and inviting, he set the alarm for four-thirty. Sleep came easily. His next recollection was reaching out of a perfect dream to stop the infernal buzzing.

17

IAN MURDOCH would have given an eyetooth for a cup of black coffee. Unfortunately, he'd slept in and was in a hurry as he turned down Bay Street toward the lake. Even then, the only available parking space was at the Pavilion. Two obviously unmarked cruisers were perched among the construction equipment. Most of the remaining parking lots had been torn up for the new Wharf Project. He could see Lou Howard and two others waiting at one end of the floating docks. Ian recognized the uniformed officer from the previous day, but the woman wearing denim jeans and jacket was a surprise.

"Detective Sergeant Logan," Murdoch acknowledged. "It's a little early to see you, isn't it?"

She shook Ian's hand with a strong grip. "Well, Inspector Murdoch, I heard you were getting an early start and thought it was worth joining you. Hope you don't mind, but Matt seemed to think it was a good idea."

"Matt?"

"I tried to reach you last night, but your cell phone was off. So I called Lou. He said you were going out to the crime scene this morning and I just invited myself along. My orders are to lead this investigation, after all, and let you contribute your expertise where needed. If that's what Matt wants, that's what he gets."

Hearing her casually refer to her most senior officer by his first name brought out an uncontrollable urge to intimidate. The last thing Ian needed was someone looking over his shoulder, and a woman no less. He was still recovering from the last woman he'd worked with.

Janna Logan smiled in response. She climbed into the waiting police boat and produced four cups, a thermos and a box.

"I bought a dozen doughnuts at Timmy's on my way into town. Let's all get a king-size sugar hit while we go up the lake."

With the boat at full throttle it was impossible to speak normally until they reached the Narrows. As they throttled down Janna Logan said, "I worked two summers at the old Muskoka Sands while going to McMaster. I once swam from the Inn to the lighthouse on a bet. It took me two and a half hours, but I won a six-pack of Molson's and ten bucks."

She turned her head and pointed as they passed the beautiful old lighthouse, just visible in the early morning mist.

"That's where I landed," she told Murdoch and Howard. Murdoch didn't doubt that she could repeat the feat if necessary. While she carefully poured coffee and passed it around, he had a chance to observe her within the confines of the boat. Ian guessed Logan to be early thirties, with short blonde hair that curled and twisted in the wind. Her jeans were tight around her shapely hips and legs and she wore a pale blue T-shirt under a police-issue windbreaker. He looked at her loafers—they were expensive. The box of doughnuts and cup of steaming coffee she handed Ian came with a smile full of near-perfect teeth. For a brief moment he recalled Caitlin's smile, far from perfect but dazzling beyond belief. He frowned at the realization that his wife had slipped his mind, only to return as sharp as the lingering pain in his leg.

By the time they reached Peter Crawford's dock the coffee and sugar hit had dissipated. Yellow crime scene tape hung around the blackened, burned-out cottage. Janna Logan was the first to speak as they stood looking at the remains of the old Muskoka cottage.

"What's the Fire Marshal come up with?"

"The written report won't be finished until samples have been analyzed in Toronto," Lou responded. "The Marshal said it's definitely arson, though, originating in different places throughout the cottage. That's why I couldn't get near the place. It was designed to be fast and effective."

Ian moved to where the body had been. Peter Crawford hadn't been positively identified yet, but Ian was sure that's who had died there. He held Janna's arm, cautioning her to walk carefully along floorboards that had burned right through in spots. She shot him a look, implying that chivalry was unnecessary and out of place. Ian shrugged and pointed to where the body was found. Some of the floorboards, where protected by the body, remained intact.

"The denseness of the body stopped the fire from completely charring the remains of his left hand. Three fingers had the tips crushed by some kind of clamping device."

"And that's the link between these two cases," Janna Logan finished for him, her eyes sparkling.

"That and the fact that this property belonged to our first victim."

"So, torture was used to extract information, but to what purpose? The reason must be on this island."

"Or was on this island," Ian said. "They wouldn't have killed Crawford and then burned the cottage if they hadn't obtained whatever they were looking for. I think that's a reasonable assumption. So, aren't you supposed to tell me what kind of person would be capable of two murders and a very professional job of arson?"

Lou Howard overheard Ian's challenge and recognized the friction between the two homicide investigators. It was time to interrupt.

"I was first on the scene. Like I said, the place was so hot I couldn't get near the building. I tried to look in, but I was afraid the window glass would blow out in my face. I ran down to the dock to see if anyone was there and found Crawford's boat still tied up. I called the fire in on my cell phone, and then alerted Albert Cowan to have his pumperboat ready. About twenty minutes later I got a call that two people had slammed into Twin Rocks. You know the story from there."

"To answer your question, Ian." Janna responded, ignoring Lou's attempt at conciliation. "The person that did this is a pro, probably male, perhaps with military experience. He knows how to extract information with a minimum of trauma but he isn't afraid to go all the way if necessary, as with Mrs. Crawford or our victim here. I'd like you, Ian, and Lou, to think back to when you came here to tell Crawford that his mother had been murdered. Do you see anything different, other than the cottage? Close your eyes and picture the area as it was that day—is there anything out of place?"

"You know, Janna, I think you have something. Remember, Lou? There was a pile of rocks right over there that I thought he was collecting to build a fire pit. Now they're scattered all over the place." Ian patted Janna on the shoulder, and immediately regretted his action. "Nothing like a fresh pair of eyes."

The young marine officer called Lou to a clump of junipers a short distance away, pointing to a paper bag hidden under the bush.

"Good for you, kid," Lou said. "You haven't touched it, have you? Maybe the lab can still pull some prints."

"What have you got?" called Logan.

"It looks like it's a Liquor Control Board bag. If he used alcohol as an accelerant, the bottles could have been in this." He carefully placed and sealed it in a plastic evidence bag.

Logan continued to poke around the burned out building while Murdoch and Howard walked the perimeter of the charred ruins.

"When Peter Crawford spent the night on my island, he said he'd just bought that boat and trailer." Lou watched Murdoch as he calculated out loud. "They must be worth at least ten thousand dollars. We think he sold coins for thirty thousand, so that leaves approximately twenty thousand bucks, give or take a couple grand for daily expenses. Albert Cowan said he paid for his repairs with American dollars."

"So, this could have been a robbery. On the other hand, it may have been suicide, the result of depression after paying someone to kill his mother." Logan had backed away and was cleaning her shoes on the grass.

"But what for? If he was going to sell another three hundred thousand worth of coins, he didn't need money did he? It doesn't add up. Robbery? I don't know. Who would know he had that kind of money in the first place?" Lou kept shaking his head, either in doubt or as an effort to avoid the lingering whiffs of smoke. "Unless ..."

"Unless the coins weren't his to begin with." The conversation had taken a turn to fully engage Murdoch.

Logan spoke from the opposite side of the remains, the morning sun rising at her back. "There's something fishy about this, Lou. We should conduct a search of a fifty-yard radius of the ruins. Look for anything out of place or foreign to the terrain, starting with that pile of rocks. Between you and the Fire Marshal, I think it's what we won't find that'll be most important."

Lou Howard looked at Murdoch, the question evident in his expression.

"C'mon, Lou, it's pretty obvious. If you're going to make a big deal from selling gold coins, what's the first thing you need?"

"Connections?"

"Gold coins," Logan interjected. "I'll get the search started."

"Meanwhile, I have to check in with that Irish mother before he calls me," Ian whispered to Lou as they walked toward the dock. "Sometimes I think he blames me personally for all the money we're spending investigating murders in Muskoka."

Ian punched Finnerty's number into his cell phone and smiled at Lou. "At least now, I can put some of the blame on Janna Logan."

Howard smiled and wandered to the shoreline, staring into the distance.

"Well now, if it isn't my favourite inspector," Finnerty

boomed when he picked up on the first ring. "It's about time you called. I had to hear about a fire, a body and a damned boating fatality from that asshole Chas Hopper. He rushed straight into the boss's office to interview him and stopped here on his way back just to gloat."

Finnerty's impatience with office politics and media hacks like Hopper was glaringly evident. He wasn't in a good mood.

"There's some fink in that district office feeding Hopper information that should come through Logan. This isn't the first time someone's upstaged me, but enough of that prick. Fill me in."

Ian explained what he knew, including Crawford's pending coin sale. He gave the few details he knew of the boating accident: one male dead, one male with minor injuries, one boat and motor smashed to shit. He carefully left his main suspicion out. Murdoch was certain that the fire and boat accident were connected. His interviews with Xiomara de Sa and Orby Lintz had crystallized the thought.

Logan called from an area at the north side of the ruins and he disconnected before Matt could ask any questions.

"Look at that," Howard growled, indicating the four empty vodka bottles at Logan's feet. "This is the kind of poison I buy when my wife's family comes to visit—nothing but pure alcohol. It doesn't leave much of a residue after a fire, I've been told. If this was used as an accelerant, the arsonist's prints may still be on them."

"We could be onto something, but don't tell the Fire Marshal yet. If he wants them, he can wait until our lab's finished with them." There was excitement in Janna Logan's voice.

"Lou, can you have someone drop me at Gravenhurst? I'll get these off to Orillia right now."

"If they get any prints, let's compare them with the set we shipped to the FBI," Ian suggested. "See if our American friends can shed some light on this."

They walked to the dock in the early morning light, a lazy fog hanging on the water. Ian was tempted to plunge straight into the cool, crystal water of Lake Muskoka. Instead, he rinsed sweat and smoke from his neck and face, then stumbled over boats stacked against the dock to the waiting police vessel. Logan leaned over the gunwales and dunked her head straight in. The cooling wind as they skimmed across the lake was heavenly.

Only moments after reaching the wharf, Janna raced off to Orillia. Ian's cell phone rang in his hand. It was Finnerty.

"What's the idea of hanging up on me?" the Superintendent barked, unwilling to miss an opportunity to needle his friend. "What did you guys find?"

"Probably the accelerant used to start the fire. I don't know, but all of this, the fire and charred body, the boat accident and the murder of Peter Crawford's mother, they're all linked together. The common thread is a guy named Orby Lintz, an associate or possible bodyguard of Jose de Sa, the man killed in the boat. I had a very superficial interview with him and we'll make sure he hangs around until the inquest, at least. That'll keep him here until we have the autopsy report for the fire victim."

"Of course, you've got evidence to back all this up," Finnerty prodded. "Right? It's not just divine inspiration."

"This Lintz character is smooth, Matt. You can tell by his

answers that he's been in this situation before. 'Yes, no, I don't know.' He never volunteers one detail he wasn't asked and he left lots out. He's my number one suspect."

"I'll take that as a no. Back to divine inspiration, then?"

"I'll admit there's one big piece of this jigsaw missing—"

"What do you mean, one big piece? Fill me in," Matt interrupted.

"As always, the question is why? All I have now is a theory and I've known you long enough not to tell you that," Ian shot back.

"I thought you'd say something like that," Finnerty laughed. And then, for good measure, he hung up on Murdoch.

Entering the hospital by the back door, Ian found the Coroner speaking into a microphone hanging over the stainless steel table supporting the charred remains of a human being. When he saw Murdoch, the doctor said, "We have a positive on the identification of the body. It's Peter Crawford. A dentist in town treated him for a root canal three years ago and she had a full X-ray of his upper jaw. The tips of the three fingers on the left hand were crushed almost like they were put in a vice. Cause of death was a broken neck. There's no indication in the lungs that he was breathing when the fire started. The person that broke his neck was a powerful man. See here, the spinal cord was wrenched almost in half."

"You examined Mrs. Crawford, as well. Are the marks on her fingers consistent with those on her son's hand?"

"It's difficult to determine. The blunt trauma to this hand wasn't identical to Mrs. Crawford's but I'd say yes, they are very similar."

Ian indicated that he'd heard enough. He was certain that

whoever murdered the mother had also murdered the son. Now that Jose de Sa was dead, the only one left on Murdoch's radar was Orby Lintz. Ian's gut feeling from the very first was that he was capable of murder. He decided to go over every detail of the case with Janna, conveniently leaving out his romantic interlude with Xiomara the previous night.

Despite his initial feelings, Ian was impressed with Janna Logan. She listened intently to what he was saying and her blue eyes flashed while he spoke. He was beginning to warm to her. She just might be some help to him, he decided, if she knew the full story.

Maybe, just maybe, Finnerty had a good idea putting her on the case.

18

ORBY LINTZ THOUGHT FOR A LONG TIME before making the call. The local cops might act stupid, but he still wasn't about to make a dumb move. He'd kept himself clean all these years by never underestimating his enemies. The call was made from a payphone in the restaurant across the road, where it couldn't be traced back to his hotel.

Manuel Ortiz had been Jose de Sa's lawyer ever since the old man had arrived in Boca Raton, Florida. Actually, de Sa had contacted him on the recommendation of a friend in Brazil. Ortiz kept a low profile, avoiding the attention that palatial offices in Mizner Square would afford. He worked from a nondescript two-storey building to the west of Dixie and south of Glades Road, with a covered parking area in rear and a keyed entrance. His discretion was exactly why clients liked dealing with Manuel Ortiz's legal firm. His clients could conduct their business in privacy, and Ortiz was careful in both scheduling and the construction of his building, ensuring no client would see another doing business with his twelve staff members.

A secure room on the second floor served as the communications centre of the law offices. It contained a bank of computers, fax machines, videophones, printers and a state-of-the-art switchboard. Everyone working there had a secure line that could be connected to any major city in the U.S., South America or the Islands, Europe and Hong Kong. The phones were manned 24-7, year-round. This room, like all of the offices, was swept for bugs every week. Electronic surveillance had become so sophisticated since 9/11 that one person with the sole responsibility of keeping the building clean was maintained on staff.

Ortiz took the call on his private line, the conversation short and concise. He'd be in Gravenhurst the following day. That was the soonest he could arrange the charter aircraft kept on retainer at Boca Airport. Orby assured him the runway in Muskoka could take jets, being a common destination for vacationing celebrities and sports stars. It wasn't until later that Ortiz received a call from the grieving wife. Still, she sounded annoyed that he'd heard of her husband's death from Lintz first.

As Jose de Sa's lawyer, Ortiz had a lot of work to do. The network of shadow companies, the multi-layered offshore investments, and numerous questionable bank accounts used to wash money, had to be carefully hidden from prying eyes. Jose de Sa was the titular head of all these corporations, but there were many influential men around the world who were big investors in de Sa's financial empire. Very influential men, Ortiz knew. A large number were residents of Palm Beach and Boca Raton.

Once the game plan was in place, he'd assure the principals that it was business as usual. After speaking with Xiomara he double-checked his plans, accounting for any monkey wrench that air-headed widow could throw at him.

The next morning the pilot called Lintz on his cell phone. It was very convenient to clear Canadian Customs and Immigration right at Muskoka Airport. Moments later, Lintz was bracing himself against the door of his car as Ortiz's aircraft taxied to a stop.

Ortiz was first to speak. "Lintz, you look like shit. You should be in hospital."

Orby shrugged off the suggestion.

"We can talk in the car," Ortiz advised him. "You'd better take me straight to Xiomara. I want to get to her before she does something stupid, like tell the cops what you were actually doing in this jerk-off town."

Lintz tried to speak but Oritz held up his hand, "And I don't want to know what the hell would bring you all the way up to Canada." Ortiz knew exactly why they were in Muskoka, but he would never admit it to Lintz. As a lawyer, he never asked a question he didn't know the answer to, but Manuel Ortiz always maintained a degree of deniability and a door to escape through. He was a survivor.

"I've talked to the other principals of the organization and they agree with me, Lintz. We'll retain you with the same financial arrangement you enjoyed with Jose. There's one proviso, however. There must be no police investigation beyond an inquest into de Sa's death. Do you understand what I'm saying? Any investigation stops right here, in this one-horse town. If it goes further, we'll hang you out to dry. Now, take me to the grieving widow. When I finish with her I'll fly back to Florida."

They had already arrived at the resort before Lintz had an opportunity to respond. Ortiz climbed immediately out of the car and walked quickly to the lobby where a desk clerk gave him directions, calling ahead to Xiomara's room to announce her visitor.

Xiomara de Sa hurried to the bathroom, steadying her shaking hand to put on her lipstick. The control she felt when she first called her new lawyer in Boca Raton had completely escaped her. She was frightened. She knew Manuel Ortiz well, a short, fat, bald Cuban-American with penetrating eyes, who'd been to dinner at their home in Boca every month. Their conversations had only ever been small talk, for her benefit, but after dinner in Jose's office for Cuban cigars and brandy, the real business discussions started. She'd overheard enough to be very cautious around Manuel Ortiz. Xiomara always made a point of retiring to her bedroom suite when he was around. Sometimes, meetings between Ortiz and Jose would last until daybreak.

Xiomara knew Ortiz disliked her. His attitude showed he only regarded her as one of Jose de Sa's assets. The feeling was mutual, of course. She'd always considered him to be subservient to her husband, as well. But, now that Jose was gone, she wasn't sure what to think. After murmuring brief and superficial condolences, Ortiz went straight to the business at hand.

"First, I don't want to know why you and your husband were here. Further, I want to caution you that no one else must know why you were here. It would be best if you even deny knowing Orby Lintz, as well. Do I make myself clear?" Ortiz looked into her eyes and struck fear in her heart.

Somehow she mustered the nerve to tell him she'd hired a lawyer in Florida to handle probate of her husband's will, although she'd never tell him whose advice she had taken.

"You did what?" Ortiz almost shouted. Xiomara jumped with fright. "Do you know what you're doing? It's your prerogative to hire your own lawyer, but first let me fill you in on a few details. Specifically about the will and provisions of your husband's estate." Ortiz made no secret of the sarcasm in his voice and accompanied it with a toothy smile. "The financial arrangement will no doubt keep you in the style to which you are presently accustomed.

"The house in Royal Palm, the furnishings, the two cars and the boat are yours, free and clear. Your membership to the Royal Palm Golf and Yacht Club will be paid in advance for ten years, plus provisions for any future assessments. You'll receive two million dollars yearly, tax-free, for a period of ten years and at the end of that time you will receive a cash settlement of twenty million dollars. At that time, all financial arrangements will cease. Unless of course ..."

Xiomara had stopped crying, desperate to show this obnoxious little man that she could be strong. She knew there had to be a catch, and she was waiting for it. Her husband's lawyer continued.

"If you have an independent lawyer represent you, you'll open a box of rotten fish. The smell will spread from the Keys to Palm Beach, and all of your close friends in Boca will end up holding their noses. Uncle Sam will have his relentless Internal Revenue Service people look into every aspect of your dear, departed husband's estate. They'll put a freeze on all monies and you'll be lucky if they give you enough to eat at Taco Bell. They'll keep you in court for the next ten years, at least, while they look into your husband's finances. Oh yes, and a few of your close friends at the Golf Club won't look too kindly on you. And that, believe it or not, is the good news."

Xiomara flopped on the couch, dropping her head in her shaking hands. She thought of calling Ian for advice, but that would be a stupid thing to do with Ortiz right there. She jumped at the slap of papers being thrown onto the coffee table.

"Mrs. de Sa, you have one minute to call your new lawyer and fire him. Then you can sign these papers and I'm out of here. I have a jet waiting at the airport to take me to Florida. If you sign, I'll put my team to work on the probate of your husband's will and I can assure you everything will go smoothly. If you decide otherwise, I'll see you in court no doubt, or jail. Whichever comes first."

Ortiz dropped his gold pen on top of the papers and indicated where she was to sign.

"Doesn't my signature need to be witnessed?" Xiomara wiped tears from her eyes.

Ortiz went into the hall where he immediately found a chambermaid. He explained that all she had to do was witness a signature on a legal document. The maid was reluctant at first, but by the time Ortiz stuffed a hundred-dollar bill in her apron pocket she'd have signed anything he asked.

When the legal documentation was duly signed and a call had been made to Xiomara's estate lawyer in Florida, Ortiz said, "I've made arrangements with McDougall's Funeral Home in Gravenhurst. They'll fly your husband's body home. His will clearly states his wish to be cremated in Boca. When you get back home, arrangements for a memorial service at the Club will already be made, a first-class tribute. Food, open bar, all that stuff. The freeloaders will show up, I'm sure.

"You did the right thing, Xiomara. This way you'll have no headaches with the IRS and you can go on living the life you're accustomed to. If you'd gone the other route, you'd be in shit up to your earlobes."

Almost as an afterthought, Ortiz placed an envelope on the coffee table.

"There's three thousand dollars in there. And two credit cards. Just sign the back and they're active. Cut up the cards you carry now. They were in your husband's name and are now cancelled. The cards have a maximum limit of twenty-five thousand each. Whatever you spend will be paid and deducted from your annual allowance."

Ortiz stuffed the stack of papers in his briefcase, abruptly shook hands and, before she could fully digest what he'd said, was gone.

19

ALTHOUGH IT WAS MIDDAY, the room was completely dark. Orby Lintz had pulled the blinds tightly closed and placed the Do Not Disturb sign on the door. He lay on the bed, fully clothed. Staring upward, trying to work his arm back and forth through the excruciating pain, he watched a spider walk across the ceiling.

Earlier, he'd looked in the bathroom mirror, surprised to find his bruising, at first almost black, was gradually turning to a sickly yellow from shoulder to waist. His ribcage was still too painful to touch and it hurt when he turned his head from one side to the other.

It had all happened so fast. When they'd hit the rocks he'd been thrown immediately and violently into the water. He couldn't even remember getting back to the smashed boat. Now he tried to recall where the gold coins were. Jose de Sa, moaning and groaning, pinned against the cockpit, the guy who came to his rescue, the boat lying in pieces on the rocks, it was all a jumble of mental images. Lintz desperately tried to recall if the fishing tackle box had remained in the boat, but couldn't remember seeing it anywhere. He came to the conclusion it had gone overboard with him when they came to a crashing stop on the unforgiving rocks.

He lay there, playing it like a slow-motion video in his mind. It had seemed only a few minutes before rescuers arrived and hauled him in. They had taken him back to the wreck where they found de Sa. Lintz had known right away the old man had bought it. Searching his memory, he was sure the tackle box wasn't where he'd placed it when they'd left Rankin Island.

Taking out the map of Lake Muskoka that he'd purchased earlier, he checked water depth around Twin Rocks, noting it went from a shelf of just fifteen feet to as much as ninety. He needed help. Reluctantly he reached for his cell phone.

It rang eight times but he wasn't concerned. He knew Steve Roman was never without his cell and would answer it, eventually. Roman, short for Romanchuck, was a commercial pilot and had a streak of larceny a mile wide. He wasn't averse to performing a shady deal if the money was right. Lintz had used him on many occasions. Roman had access to an aircraft, was capable of flying fast distances and, best of all, his hobby was skin diving. He was exactly what Lintz needed right now.

Roman also had some costly habits—booze, broads and cocaine. His stable of female companions at Miami's South Beach were drop-dead gorgeous, willing, and expensive. His bankroll, Lintz knew, was depleting fast. Steve Roman always needed money and, when he finally answered, he was eager to hear what Orby wanted of him.

Lintz gave Roman the barest of details, figuring the less he knew the better. He needed him as soon as possible at Muskoka Airport in Ontario, Canada—with vest, fins, regulator and all the necessary gear for diving in a hundred feet of water, Lintz stipulated. If necessary, they could pick up additional air tanks from the dive shop in Gravenhurst.

The next call Lintz made was to de Sa's widow. His purpose was to shake her up, put the fear of God in her so she wouldn't say anything to the cops. He took a sadistic delight in rattling her cage. In no way could she be allowed to indicate any connection between her husband's fishing trip and the fire on Rankin Island. Hanging up on her a few moments later, Lintz considered his position and decided that, yes, with a little control, a chance at de Sa's stash of coins was well worth the effort.

Steve Roman was about as much in control as his habits. Expenses had increased so much that he couldn't rely on Orby Lintz as his only source of income. He had to keep as many irons in the fire as possible to support his lifestyle. When he finished speaking with Lintz, he speed-dialled another number, one that was immediately answered. The person on the other end knew exactly why Lintz wanted Roman in Canada, and why the diving gear would be necessary. It was then that Steve Roman first heard about the million dollars' worth of gold coins, causing him to nearly drop the phone. Even a small percentage of that would buy a lot of white powder. Listening to his newest instructions, Roman swallowed twice before responding.

"Okay, you can rely on me to do the job." The phone went dead in his hand but he couldn't stop staring at it like it was a living, breathing thing. Finally, he gathered his wits and set about his preparations. The aircraft would have to be serviced and readied. All the documentation and filings for an international flight plan to Muskoka and return would be required. He'd need to cover his tracks. After careful consideration he routed himself through several airports, showing his origin as Laredo, Texas, a town on the Mexican border.

Manuel Ortiz was worried. This damned gold coin thing was getting out of hand. He had to put a lid on it. With de Sa dead, the partners nervous, and that sociopath Lintz wanting to retrieve the coins, there was too much that could go wrong. Steve Roman, he hoped, was the man to complete this phase. If not, and if the Ontario Provincial Police were to find the gold and make a few easy connections, this world-class police force could cripple the whole organization. Ortiz knew from experience that even cash wouldn't deflect the Canadian police.

Ortiz had closed the door on de Sa's widow. She was a money-grabbing bitch, and a bit of a lame-brain, so a few million dollars would keep her content until an appropriate opportunity came to dispose of her. In the meanwhile, she'd be no problem. Steve Roman had become Plan A, now it was up to the lawyer to organize Plan B. With multiple millions at stake, previously laundered and distributed by Jose de Sa, the organization would now consider Ortiz their point man. The principals relied upon him to keep their identities secret and the enormous wealth generated by the cartel flowing. Failure was never an option, Manuel Ortiz knew, and the full power of the organization would be brought to bear, ensuring mistakes were dealt with expeditiously. When he finalized his Plan B, it would completely shut down the ramifications of de Sa's obsession, diverting attention from the gold, and allowing them to get back to business.

20

THE CALL FROM LINTZ had a spectacular effect. Xiomara was coming unglued again. She thought of Ian Murdoch and wondered why he hadn't called. Could she tell him that Lintz had more or less threatened her? Her life was in danger, but the possibility that her indirect involvement might implicate her as an accessory was every bit as worrisome. She searched her luggage for the other cell phone, the one she kept hidden from everyone.

A side door from the hotel led to the parking lot. She found the rental car, entered the front passenger door and punched in the number, long fingernails clicking on the plastic casing of the miniature phone. It buzzed five times at the other end, followed by four familiar clicks that were her signal to speak. When she first trained to use this phone she couldn't get used to talking to a machine that monitored and recorded her messages. In the event of an emergency, she was never sure there was someone to hear her. There always was, of course. Quickly she related her story: the gold coins, the burned cottage, the murdered bank clerk, Orby Lintz and finally Manuel Ortiz. She gave Ian Murdoch's name as the investigating OPP officer. When she was done she felt drained of emotion, completely unnerved. Was someone really listening? If what the lawyer, Ortiz, had told her about an IRS investigation of her husband's estate was true, she could be left penniless. But she had no alternative—being an accomplice to murder was a far greater risk than the possibility of being broke. Although she was reluctant to call, this was payback time, time to atone for what she'd done in the past.

The CIA had recruited her when she was a young, struggling fashion model. Her career took her to photo shoots all over the world and a CIA handler had sold her on the opportunity to do her duty for her adopted country. It was a bill of goods she soon decided was just so much bullshit. What she could tell her handler about money laundering, drug trades and arms smuggling wasn't apparent to her. The information she supplied was practically nil and it soon became more interesting to snort a few lines and carry drugs through customs for ever more demanding friends, with the protection and unwitting assistance of the CIA. It had been fun, at first, until someone discovered that information was being passed on. Her habits and favours had kept her beyond suspicion, but the seriousness of it all came home to her dramatically when she discovered her roommate, a beautifully wraithlike and wonderful friend, dead of an overdose. Gisele had never used drugs, had never a bad word to say about anyone. The message was clear—her suppliers had thought Gisele was the informant.

Horrified, Xiomara had quit the modelling business and cleaned herself up. For two years she thought she was through with all of the nonsense, until a few months after she married Jose de Sa. She'd been at the Town Centre shopping complex in Boca Raton when her former handler approached in the parking lot of Saks Fifth Avenue. He wanted her to spy on her husband.

Xiomara flatly refused. To be a mole in her own home was

abhorrent to her, country or no country. She soon discovered, however, that marriage to Jose was little more than a name on a legal document and a handsome expense account. She wasn't privy to her husband's business activities, had absolutely no influence on the running of her own home, and was seldom permitted any decisions beyond purchases of personal items. To compensate, she made sure that all of her purchases were substantial.

The agent, unfortunately, kept coming back, appearing in restaurants and dance clubs until, finally fed up with being little more than a fixture in her own home, she gave in. Xiomara agreed that she'd pass along names of people who visited her husband. The Agency was especially interested in those present when Manuel Ortiz was also at her home. It was her home, after all, and Ortiz was a thoroughly detestable man. What could be wrong with supplying a little information?

21

THERE WAS ONLY ONE PERSON in the boat as it slowed through the Narrows. Then, at full speed, it raced toward Twin Rocks where it came to an abrupt stop on the southwest corner of the protruding granite. The anchor dropped and the craft swung southerly against the rope, reacting to a slight breeze. It would be completely dark within the hour, the eastern shore already in shadow. The boat was barely visible from cottages in the distance.

The sole occupant, dressed in a diving suit, climbed over the side. He wore fins, mask and snorkel, and carried a flashlight as he disappeared into the depths of the lake.

Within minutes the diver re-emerged, a mere ten feet from the bow. He heaved a box into the bottom of the boat then quickly hauled himself in, raised anchor and coasted astern. Once a reasonable distance had grown between the boat and Twin Rocks, he sped at top speed toward a nearby island. In the lowering light, the boat had no running lights and darkness swallowed up the lake. The only things visible were the twinkling of cottage lights.

At the island, he stayed for only a matter of minutes. Soon enough the lone figure let go the lines to the dock, made sure the running lights were off, and slowly made way for Twin Rocks again, where he momentarily drifted along the southern shoal. The evening quiet was briefly interrupted by the soft splash of the box as it returned to the lake.

The engine coughed, then came to life. In the open lake at last the running lights went on and, at full throttle, the vessel sped into the night.

22

IAN MURDOCH called Matt Finnerty from his room at Taboo.

"I've been trying to reach you," Matt barked. "Your cell phone battery gone dead? I was anxious to know how you're getting along with Janna Logan. She's one smart gal—and she also spent two years on the FBI's elite Serial Crime Unit at Quantico. This kid's no lightweight, Ian. Was she any help?"

"She was some help," Ian reluctantly agreed. "But no barn burner. What I wanted to talk to you about, though, was the Coroner's Inquest into the Jose de Sa accident."

"De Sa? Hold on a minute …" Ian could hear the soft click of a computer keyboard over the line and wondered how an old warhorse like Finnerty had found time to master current technology. "Okay, I've got him. Jose de Sa, formerly of Boca Raton, Florida. He had a trophy wife about half his age. Seems like your Mr. de Sa was very old, very rich, and is now very dead following an accident on Lake Muskoka. He made the mistake of letting some guy named Lintz drive the boat. Now what does he have to do with the Crawford inquiry?"

"Simple, Matt. Where would a guy like Peter Crawford find several hundred thousand dollars in gold coins?"

"From someone old and rich."

"Exactly. You know my theory that both Crawford's deaths are linked, that's pretty obvious. According to my father, the coin dealer he works for was arranging to purchase approximately three hundred thousand dollars worth of coins from Peter Crawford. Assuming Crawford financed his new boat and holiday the same way, this kid probably had a lot more than that to begin with. I'd like to know just what he's already sold and what it adds up to."

Ian rushed to continue before Finnerty could interrupt.

"This would have been at least the second time Crawford sold some coins. I believe Orby Lintz purchased the coins back from the dealer, either on his own or on de Sa's behalf. I'd like you to send a cruiser down to the coin dealer in Toronto, see if we can bring him to Bracebridge to make a positive identification of Lintz. Secondly, I want you to stall the de Sa inquest for seventy-two hours. The delay will keep the major players within our jurisdiction until we can get an I.D. It should also give me time to bring this thing to a head. Whether we'll ever recover the gold is anybody's guess, but we're going through Peter Crawford's cottage property with a fine-tooth comb. We also had a barge take the pieces of de Sa's rental boat to the Fire College. There was no trace of coins in it, but it's still part of a fatal accident inquiry so we'll be holding it anyway. Lou Howard wonders if there was a third party they passed the coins to before crashing into the rocks."

"Hey," Finnerty interrupted. "He might have something there. What about de Sa's wife? Could she have the coins?"

"No way, she has an ironclad alibi." Ian was sorry he'd mentioned Howard's theory, no matter how ridiculous it seemed.

"What do you mean, ironclad? Have you questioned her?" Finnerty was probing where Ian didn't want to go. "I don't want to find out afterwards that she and Lintz were in this together."

"The hotel clerk verified it," Ian lied. "There's a possibility she never even left the hotel on the day of the accident."

"Okay. If you're sure about her, I'm happy. About the Inquest, don't worry. They won't call it for at least four days and I'll have the coin dealer in Bracebridge by noon tomorrow. Oh, by the way, Ian, try to keep Janna Logan in the loop. She could be your boss some day. They're phasing out us old bastards and replacing us with PhD's."

"No problem, Matt. When there isn't room for guys like you, me and Lou, it won't be worth sticking around."

Ian made another call to Xiomara's room. It rang six times

before an uncharacteristically husky voice answered, apologizing for the delay. She'd been sleeping, she explained, both physically and emotionally drained by events of the previous few days. She declined Ian's invitation for dinner but regained enough composure to thank him for calling.

Disappointed, Ian slammed the phone down.

"Goddamn it, I have to talk to her," he muttered.

23

STEVE ROMAN had signed the hangar's short-term lease and filed his flight plan from Boca Raton Executive Airport. A Lear 31 had the capacity to fly direct to Gravenhurst in hours, but he'd be making a detour or two to muddy the waters. It was towed to the tarmac where an attendant helped load two heavy sports bags into the cabin while Steve did his customary walk around. He led a fast and easy life, but when it came to flying he never left anything to chance.

Once inside the aircraft he opened one bag, removing both a screwdriver and a carefully wrapped oilskin bundle. Canadian Customs would clear the aircraft at Muskoka, probably without searching, but he wasn't taking chances. He went into the tiny head, the bathroom, and removed a panel from under the sink. He took an automatic pistol, a silencer and two clips of ammo from their wrapping and hid them behind the panel. Back in the cockpit he calmly began his flight check. He'd call Lintz with his ETA when he'd left Boca far behind and taken off again from Laredo.

Roman had done everything by the book. He made the

Mandatory Frequency check with London, Ontario, and requested a customs officer to clear him at Muskoka. For the international leg, his registered point of origin was listed as Sharon, Pennsylvania.

Orby Lintz's stomach was rumbling—he needed nourishment. Pulling a hair from his head, he laid it carefully on the telephone receiver. If these yokels were cute enough to tap his phone or plant a bug, they'd probably need to install it in the phone. He made sure the Do Not Disturb sign was on the door before slipping across to Kelsey's restaurant next door. Ordering a big steak, baked potato, and a Caesar that he washed down with a good Canadian beer, he was just figuring out the proper amount for an unmemorable tip when his cell phone rang. Steve Roman would be at Muskoka Airport in two hours.

Lintz called Cowan's Marina and ordered a boat for seven o'clock the next morning. He drove to Gravenhurst and rented two air tanks at the dive shop. It was a hot day but, coming from Florida, Lintz didn't mind. He drove to the local airport via District Road 17, a two-lane, lightly travelled back road, then right on 118 to the parkway leading south to the airport entrance. He regularly checked his rearview mirrors to be sure he wasn't followed.

Orby Lintz had to admit that he needed Steve Roman. The pain of his injuries had eased when he walked but he was still in no shape to go into the water looking for the tackle box. Lost in thought, he heard the jet approaching from the clear sky only at the last minute.

Roman taxied in and parked. When Customs had cleared him, he unloaded the sport bags. Lintz was of no help in lifting the dive equipment into the trunk of his car.

"Fucking hell, Orby, you look like death warmed over. And you're walking like an old man. De Sa dead and you all banged up, it must've been some fight."

Lintz didn't appreciate the humour.

"You're booked into the Howard Johnson's in Gravenhurst," he growled. "Be ready by six-thirty tomorrow morning and I'll fill you in on the details. I don't want the local cops putting you and me together, so I'm staying ten miles away in Bracebridge."

At his hotel, Roman retrieved the small case that held his clothes and shaving gear from the trunk of Lintz's car. After checking in, he thumbed through the Yellow Pages to find a car rental agency. They were out of cars but had a pick-up truck they could deliver in a half hour.

From memory he retraced the route to the airport, going straight to the Lear and opening the head. He retrieved the oilskin package from behind the panel and waited while the craft was refuelled. When it was completed he paid the tanker driver in cash.

There were two hours of daylight left. He used the time to familiarize himself with the layout of Gravenhurst, enquiring after the location of Cowan's Marina from a store clerk. The drive out from town along 169 took him past a new construction development and two ships, RMS *Segwun* and *Wenonah II*. Their antiquated shapes and sizes intrigued him. A tourism brochure informed him the *Segwun* was over a hundred years old and the only remaining coal-fired steam vessel operating in North America. Steve Roman was impressed, but his curiosity had to be kept in check. He had other work to do.

A cursory examination of the lay of Cowan's Marina was sufficient. The next job was to familiarize himself with Taboo, the resort where Xiomara de Sa was staying. Manuel Ortiz had given him the room number and he checked visibility and distance from fire exits, parking lots and the main entrance. There was security in a booth at the Beach Road entrance, out of sight of the hotel proper. The sole exit was through an unmanned automatic turnstile. Dealing with the lawyer in Florida, he knew, meant that you couldn't afford any slip-ups. Ortiz had a very long arm, as Orby Lintz was about to discover.

Steve Roman noticed headlines in the local papers in the lobby of the hotel. He picked up several, discarding most as junk. Of the two he kept, both had full-page stories detailing the fire on Rankin Island and discovery of a body at the scene. Foul play was suspected, they announced, but police were unforthcoming with information. The surprising fact was that Isobel Crawford's murder, although prominently mentioned, wasn't directly linked to the unidentified burn victim. Ortiz had given him a quick briefing, but somehow the bastard had passed none of this on.

He called Ortiz in Florida from his room phone when he discovered he'd forgotten the battery charger for his cell in the Lear. Reading aloud the account of the two murders, Steve thought he'd never heard Ortiz so agitated. The lawyer reiterated the terms of the job Roman was hired to perform in a loud and angry voice.

"Do it, you son of a bitch. Then get out of that rock-and-trees hole as fast as you can."

There was one more chore Steve had to do. He drove the rented pick-up to the parking lot near the steamships, locked it, and walked back to Howard Johnson's.

A few minutes after six the following morning, Roman was at the rear entrance of the hotel with his small case in hand. If anything, Lintz looked worse than the previous day and Steve enjoyed telling him so. The comment was not appreciated. Lintz hadn't been able to sleep more then an hour at a time since the accident, the pain in his back and chest so intense that he couldn't relax his breathing. He looked exhausted.

While driving to the parking lot of Cowan's Marina, Orby Lintz told Roman about the tackle box he was convinced was at the bottom of the lake, hence the need for diving gear. He related how this smart-assed kid, Crawford, had diddled old man de Sa and stolen the coins. When Roman asked him about their value, Lintz became belligerent.

"None of your fucking business. You're paid to do a job and that's all." Steve Roman was pretty much sick of hearing it yet again. And again there was no mention of two highly publicized murders. He kept his mouth shut. Lintz was a single-minded son of a bitch, probably never read papers or watched local TV, so there was a small chance he hadn't even seen the local accounts. He'd know all about them firsthand, Roman was absolutely sure. He'd seen Orby Lintz operate before.

Albert Cowan helped Steve carry the air tanks and bags to their boat. Steve placed his small case under one of them near the bow while Lintz gave Albert three hundred dollars in American cash, more than enough for four hours rental. Albert still didn't look thrilled.

"Just try to bring this one back, will ya?"

Steve removed his shirt and pants before getting into the boat, putting on his wetsuit vest. He felt the water, a little cold for his liking, but decided not to wear the full suit. The morning mist had nearly cleared from the lake and it promised to be a fine day. Away from the marina, Lintz steered down the channel between the shore and Rankin Island. He was careful to reduce speed and trim the boat to keep Twin Rocks visible over the bow. Once there, he circled several times, trying to recall exactly where he and de Sa had slammed into them. At last he stopped to drift at the south point of the rocks, telling Roman to throw out the anchor.

Steve cinched up his vest, attached hoses to the air tanks and tested them, then let Lintz snap them to clips in back of the dive jacket. He put the regulator to his mouth and tested it as well. Fins strapped on and mask in place, he sat precariously on the gunwale of the boat before falling backward into the water. He came up immediately.

"Holy shit, that water's cold. I'll have to put on the rest of the wet suit." Steve shivered, holding the regulator in his hand.

"Never mind the rest of the suit, you pussy. It'll only take a few minutes to find the box, so stay where you are." Lintz was staring threateningly into his eyes over the side of the boat.

Roman descended while Orby watched the path of bubbles breaching the surface. After several long minutes he banged the side of the hull, signalling to Roman that he was searching in the wrong place. Lintz pointed just off the stern of the anchored boat where, through the greenish-blue water, Steve located the box. It was laying on its side, down deep. He swam over and asked Lintz for the weight belt before diving. To a southern boy, the water at that depth was freezing cold. Eventually he managed to grab the handle of the box and return to the surface.

Lintz, moaning in pain, had great difficulty lifting the heavy fishing box full of water into the bottom of the boat. Roman wasted no time getting back in and didn't even bother to strip off or towel down, his curiosity at seeing a million dollars in gold more intense than his drop in body temperature.

Lintz wasn't about to wait patiently while Steve stowed his dive gear and dressed, either. He quickly laid the box on its side so the water drained away, then righted it, flicked open the two latches and raised the lid. His curse startled nearby gulls into flight and could be heard on shore.

"Son of a bitch!" He turned the box over and a pile of rocks spilled onto the deck. "That fucking bitch! That lousy, fucking bitch," he swore, again and again. "Her and that dumbassed cop, they made a switch while I was waiting for you to get here. There's no way they're getting away with this."

"Simmer down, Orby. How did they make a switch? Think about it, man."

"I am thinking about it. When I saw them at the hospital you could see there was something going on. I just never made the connection. She's the only one in this jerk-off town that knew about the gold." Lintz's face had turned blood red with rage. Steve thought, not without amusement, that it looked as if he would explode.

"That bitch told the cop and he came out here for the tackle box, brought it up, took out the gold and put in these fucking rocks. That cute bitch—she's as good as dead." Orby wasn't even bothering to breathe, he was speaking so fast. The look in his eyes had turned to murder.

Steve Roman's eyes betrayed no emotion at all. He calmly reached down, picked up one of the larger rocks and struck Lintz on the side of the temple. Lintz fell, his head spurting blood over the deck. Stunned, he lay along the keel while Roman raised anchor, throttled up and sped away from Twin Rocks. There was an island in the distance that would hide his boat from view. The only property in sight had a dock, but no boat tied to it. Reason dictated there couldn't be anyone on an island if they didn't have a boat. Calmly, he retrieved his automatic from the small bag, screwed on the silencer, pressed it to Orby Lintz's head and fired, confident that the extended barrel and small calibre would let the bullet bounce around in Lintz's skull. The natural inlet and surrounding trees absorbed the sound of two quick shots, dissipating them beyond recognition at any distance.

Steve Roman strapped an empty air tank and weight belt onto Lintz's lifeless body, and heaved the dead weight over the side. There was one loud splash and then Orby Lintz was no more. Lake Muskoka had swallowed up a cold-blooded murderer, the victim of his own greed.

Remembering the map of Muskoka Lake he'd seen at the Wharf, Roman took his bearings from the white lighthouse.

From there, he knew, he could easily find the entrance to the inner bay and the lot where his pick-up was parked. In the distance he spotted the white building shining in the morning sun. He turned the boat and churned up a wake, throwing out the empty box and the rocks that had spilled from it. With a small bailing bucket he scooped water into the boat, washing blood from the deck and his clothes. By the time Albert Cowan found it again, there would be no sign of either himself or Orby Lintz, and no way to trace them.

24

Ian was awakened by his cell phone. Still tired from a fitful sleep, the unfamiliarity of his room at Taboo didn't help. He pressed the phone to his ear to find the caller was Lou Howard.

"We've been watching Orby Lintz's room, but our man on the four to eight either fell asleep or was out for coffee," Lou cut straight to the chase. "Lintz's car is gone from the parking lot. Sorry, Ian. He can't be far and we've put his licence number on our watch list. If he's anywhere in the area, we should get a report soon."

"Well, we have to locate him fast," Ian responded. "A coin dealer from T.O. will be here by noon to make the I.D. What have you come up with at the LCBO stores—anyone remember our guy buying four bottles of cheap vodka?"

"Unfortunately, there's a lot of part-time help in the summer season, so we haven't spoken to all of the clerks yet. Up to now, no one remembers a face, and no one's anxious to tackle the reams of sales receipts to go through. I really can't blame them. They're busy as hell at this time of year. As far as prints on the bag go, we've got nothing we can use. Up shit creek again." For a guy that had only bad news, Lou Howard was enjoying his morning far too much.

"Meet me at the Muskoka Wharf in an hour," Ian grumbled. "I want to take another look at the crime scene on Rankin Island, and it might not be a bad idea to ask Janna Logan to come along for the ride. Those gold coins have got to be somewhere." Ian felt his beard, hoping a cold shower and shave would wake him. Then it was time for coffee and breakfast. It would give him a good start on the day, and putting it on Matt Finnerty's tab always made things look brighter. Maybe that was Lou's secret, too.

Once again, Ian had difficulty parking. By nine o'clock, spots around the Wharf construction were at a premium. He saw Howard and Logan at the end of the one of the docks. By the look on Lou's face, Murdoch guessed his day had taken a turn for the worst. Janna, by contrast, looked relaxed. She was wearing tight Chinos and a white T-shirt draped flatteringly from her shoulders.

"We've been here for twenty minutes. What kept you?" Lou barked. "You know what the mosquitoes are like over the water?"

"Taboo isn't the kind of greasy spoon you're used to," Ian laughed. "They serve breakfast like you've got all morning to eat it." Ian glanced around. "By the way, where's the chauffeur—don't you rate a driver any more?"

There was something eating Lou Howard and Ian was going to enjoy taking him over the edge. He knew Lou well and, besides, that's what old friends are for. Janna Logan remained silent—this wasn't a pissing contest she was going to get into. She sensed the two old friends might play the Ike and Mike game often.

Lou slammed the throttle full ahead and the bow of the boat rose at a steep angle before settling onto an even keel. The wind tossed Janna's hair, forcing Ian to once again find unwilling comparisons to Caitlin. He took the port seat, then leaned and shouted over the motor into Lou's ear.

"Take her around Twin Rocks first, Lou."

Howard gave him a puzzled look in response, raising both hands from the steering wheel in a querying gesture. The speed limit through the Narrows allowed Ian to explain his intentions.

"The coins have to be somewhere, don't they? If they weren't in the cottage, and if de Sa and Lintz didn't have them, I'm guessing they've got to be at the bottom around Twin Rocks. We should get a diver to search the area."

"Both of our available divers are up at Lake Temagami," Lou advised. "They've been looking for a couple of missing fishermen for a few days. I can have them here tomorrow." Lou had cooled his antagonism and appeared to be intent on Ian's theory. "Besides, I was on the scene here within fifteen minutes of the crash. I certainly didn't see any gold coins in the boat. In my opinion, Lintz and de Sa didn't have them. They're either melted into a pile of metal in that cottage, or they're hidden somewhere we'll never find them."

At Twin Rocks, Howard steered in ever-diminishing circles, manoeuvering professionally around the jagged rocks. Ian peered into the clear water but nothing was immediately visible. Frustrated, he pointed to Rankin Island in the distance and Lou took them away from the shoal before hammering down on the throttle once more.

Janna leaned over to Ian, pointing to his island. "It looks beautiful. Sea Gull Island, isn't it? You're fortunate to have such a secluded spot to unwind."

Ian nodded in response but didn't speak. Janna Logan knew a little too much about him for comfort. When they tied up at Peter Crawford's dock, Ian took Lou aside and asked, "Did you tell her that was my island?"

"Don't get your balls in a snit, Murdoch. It wasn't me." Lou was sounding pissed again.

At the cottage site, Ian walked carefully onto what was left of the floor of the burned-out hulk.

"I've got Foley Barge Service coming to pick up all this wreckage," Janna said. "I want them to take it to the Fire College where the forensic guys will go through it. The barge should be here tomorrow." She fell silent for a moment. Ian thought she'd finished when she turned directly to him.

"The Boca Raton Police checked the bank Peter Crawford worked for. There have been no thefts reported, but they did confirm that Jose de Sa was a depositor. That's not just a coincidence, if you ask me. He had two safe deposit boxes in his name and young Crawford routinely had access to them. Unfortunately, the bank won't provide more information without a court order. I couldn't give the local authorities sufficient reason to apply to a judge to open them, or even divulge how much money de Sa had in his accounts."

"I see what you're driving at," Lou said. "You suspect these gold coins were stashed away by de Sa. Then Crawford lifted them and de Sa never reported the theft. That would be a pretty good indication they're dirty."

"You've got it in one," Murdoch smiled. "I think this whole case goes a lot deeper than we initially suspected. Janna, you spent time at Quantico, you've got to have made some friends there. Any way you can get a reading about the late Jose de Sa and his friend Orby Lintz? We could institute a formal request through Orillia, but that'll take days. I've a gut feeling this whole thing is going to blow up in our face soon, and we don't have that kind of time to spare."

Howard continued to search the property until his radio squawked. He listened for a moment before responding.

"Great. Stay out of sight and we'll be there in about fifteen minutes." Lou waved to Murdoch and Logan.

"An officer has located Lintz's car at Cowan's Marina. He'll keep it under surveillance."

The three piled back into the OPP boat and Lou pushed it to the limit around the south end of Rankin Island. In the open lake he turned northeast, between Rankin and the mainland. When they were in sight of the marina he swung a wide arc, throttled down and pulled right into the covered boathouse. A uniformed officer was waiting to catch and tie the line Ian threw to him.

"Mr. Cowan says the car's been here since seven this morning. Two men rented a boat, he told me, but when I told him you were going to be here in a few minutes he said he'd fill you in personally."

As if by magic, Albert materialized in the gloom of the covered boathouse.

"My wife's always bitching at me to stay out of the sun."

Albert wiped perspiration from his forehead and neck. "It's cooler here, anyway, and we won't be disturbed. "

"We're in a hurry here," Lou barked. "Spill it, Albert."

"Well," Cowan clearly didn't like being rushed. "Two days ago a guy called, late in the afternoon. He wanted to rent a boat and insisted it needed an anchor with enough rope to get down one hundred feet. He called again the following day and ordered it for this morning. They arrived right on seven. The driver of the car looked like he'd had a regular shit kicking—could hardly walk. The other one, he was a big mother. About six-foot-three, well built and a great tan. He did all the lift and carry." Albert stopped, either to consider what he was about to say or just to piss Lou Howard off.

"Two air tanks, they had. And two big sport bags like the kind divers carry their gear in. They took off like a bat out of hell, south towards the Narrows." Albert shifted on his feet. "I hope that mother didn't smash up another boat."

"What do you mean, another boat?" Janna interrupted.

"Stay with the program," Albert laughed. "The battered-up guy was the one in the accident at Twin Rocks."

"Are you sure it was diving equipment in those bags?" Ian asked.

"Not absolutely, but why the air tanks? I don't think he was going to blow up balloons. I've seen enough of that kind of bag to say I'm ninety per cent sure."

"Anything else?" It was Janna, again.

"Oh, yeah. He paid in cash—American hundred-dollar bills."

"What kind of boat was it?" Janna enquired. Albert just looked at her, trying to figure out who she was.

"Sorry, Albert. This is Janna Logan—she's in charge of the case," Ian explained.

"Not hard to see where she learned her manners." Albert shot a glare at Lou Howard.

"All right, Albert," Lou almost apologized. "You've made your point. Now, can you answer the question?"

Albert walked them outside and over to the gas pumps where he pointed to a boat tied up alongside. "It's exactly like that one."

Ian shook Albert's hand, "Thanks again, you've been a big help. We'll get your boat back."

"Hunh," Albert Cowan spit into the oil stained water near the pumps. "Try to bring it back in one piece, will ya?"

The four police officers returned to the boathouse where their own craft was tied.

"I want you to stay here," Ian instructed the uniformed constable. "Get your patrol car out of sight and keep that rental under surveillance. If anyone so much as looks at it, call us immediately and wait for back-up." He patted the young officer on the shoulder.

"The three of us will head back to the Wharf. There's only one reason they had dive gear, and that's because they lost the coins when Lintz hit the rocks. Unfortunately, they were about an hour ahead of us this morning."

As they were about to cast off Albert came running up.

"Hey, Ian. I forgot to tell you. The big guy, his name was Steve."

"When we get to the Wharf I want to go straight to the Community Office. Lou, will you help me make some calls?" Janna was fully in charge now. "I'll contact everyone I can think of at the FBI. This thing is bigger than we thought, and all of a sudden we've got another character on the scene. Who is he, and why's he here? These coins are like a magnet. If we find them, I think we'll find our killer."

"How much do you want to bet it's Orby Lintz?" Murdoch challenged.

"What about you, Ian? What are you going to do?"

"I'm going to go question the widow," Ian sighed. A look of total concentration creased his brow.

25

XIOMARA HAD PACKED EVERYTHING into two bags, her dead husband's waiting beside hers at the door of the suite. She'd had enough of tension, unrelenting fear, and Orby Lintz. Now she just wanted to get back home to Florida as soon as possible. Her surreptitious call for help remained unanswered and Xiomara feared she was on her own. If she got out of Canada now, she felt she could at least avoid an Accessory charge in Peter Crawford's death. Even Ian Murdoch couldn't help her.

There was a gentle knock at the door. Xiomara opened it without hesitating, certain it was the bellhop. When she did, however, Steve Roman bounded in, shoving her backward. At the same time he drew his automatic, a weapon he'd concealed under his shirt while in the hallway, and pointed it. Roman looked to the bags and then back at her.

"Well, Mrs. Smart-Ass, I got here just in time. You thought you and that cop were going to get away with it, did you?

That was a cute trick, by the way, substituting rocks for the gold coins. You had Lintz totally fooled. Should have seen him when he opened that tackle box and found nothing but the rocks in there. He went ballistic, of course."

At the mention of Lintz's name, and with realization that the coins were lost, Xiomara's panic showed plainly on her face.

"Don't worry, honey. He ain't going to come after you now. You see, he's feeding the fish at the bottom of Lake Muskoka. But, before he went swimming he managed to tell me how you and that cop did it. How the hell did you talk a cop into getting in bed with you?" His toothy smile spread across his tanned face. "Or is that a stupid question?"

"I don't know what you're talking about," Xiomara put up a brave front. "Who the hell are you? And please, get that gun out of my face."

The lifeless glare Roman returned sent shivers down Xiomara's spine.

"Who I am is of no consequence. Where's the gold? Give it up now and you can be on your way."

He had Orby Lintz's eyes, calculating and merciless, and she knew instinctively that she'd never leave the room alive.

There was another knock at the door. Both she and the stranger froze.

"Mara? It's Ian Murdoch."

Steve Roman couldn't believe his luck. He'd managed to catch them both before they got away with Ortiz's loot. He pointed the gun at Xiomara's head, put his hand in the air to demand calm, then whispered in her ear.

"You be real smart, bitch. Tell him you'll be with him in

just a moment, then open the door slowly and casually. If you try to warn him, someone's going to die."

Ian came into the room, wondering at Xiomara's nervous smile, and was greeted by an automatic pistol.

Oh shit, Ian thought. Not again.

"What a pair," Roman said, whistling between his teeth. "But now that you're both here, let's make it quick and easy. Which bag has the coins? Just point it out and I'll be out of here. Make no mistake, cop, I didn't fly all the way up here to be diddled by some greedy yokel who was taken in by a gorgeous broad. Who the hell did you think you were dealing with?"

Ian shot a quick glance of disbelief at Xiomara. Goddamn it, had another woman duped him? For his stupidity he was about to get his head blown off.

"You've got it all wrong," Ian said, biding for time. "I'm not her accomplice, and we don't have the coins. It's Orby Lintz you should be looking for."

"Orby Lintz, you dumb-ass, is dead. Now, let's try this one more time. Where's the money?" He'd pulled the silencer out of his back pocket and was about to thread it onto the muzzle of the automatic.

"Dead? Then I guess that means you're Steve. I've heard of you." Ian was playing it by ear. He needed time to think and, judging by the quick look Steve gave him, he might have gone too far.

"I don't know what kind of game you're playing, but it's time to stop the horseshit. Which bag has the coins?" Roman was waving the gun in the direction of the suitcases. Frightened beyond thought, Xiomara didn't know what else to do. She pointed to her husband's bag.

Roman instructed Ian to lift it onto the bed and open it. As he did, noting its weight, Murdoch caught a glimpse of Xiomara's eyelids fluttering rapidly. He wasn't sure exactly what she was trying to tell him, but he guessed the coins weren't in the bag. Just then there was yet another loud knock at the door. A cheerful voice called from the hallway.

"Pick up your bags, Mrs. de Sa?"

"Don't answer that," Roman whispered.

"But I called for a bellhop to carry my bags to the car," she pleaded.

"Okay, let him in. Give him your car keys and the other bag, but leave that one here." Roman waved his free hand at Jose de Sa's expensive holdall on the bed. "If either one of you makes a dumb move, I'll kill everyone. Now, very slowly, let him in."

Opening the door, Xiomara explained to the uniformed bellhop that her white Cadillac was parked at the end of the first row just outside the door. "Leave the keys on the seat," she told him, and reached to offer a folded bill for a tip.

Back in the hallway, with the door closed behind him, the bellhop took a few steps before casually looking at his gratuity. He was struck dumb. It was an American hundred-dollar bill.

26

JANNA LOGAN called her FBI contact in Virginia from the Community Police Office in Gravenhurst. "Mr. Jacks isn't available at this time," a recorded voice stated. "Please leave a short message and immediate number where you may be reached. Your call will be returned within fifteen minutes." She'd hardly put down the receiver when the call came back.

Making a clear and concise report, Janna advised Jacks that two murders in Gravenhurst, Ontario, could have American connections. As far as she knew, Orby Lintz was definitely suspected, an American citizen named Jose de Sa was dead, and de Sa's wife, Xiomara, might also be implicated.

At a rear desk, out of earshot of others, she wrote feverishly with the receiver cradled in the crook of her neck. Her eyes flashed across her notes before she read her shorthand back to Jacks. Satisfied that her transcription was accurate, she thanked the agent profusely.

Janna found PC Babcock doing routine paperwork with a deceptively calm view of Bay Street. Quickly explaining her work with Murdoch and Howard, she emphasized the urgency of the matter. She needed two officers, immediately, at Muskoka Airport. There, according to Agent Jacks, they'd find a Lear jet on the tarmac.

"Allow no one near it and be sure to proceed with caution," she advised him. "Anyone who approaches the aircraft should be regarded as armed and dangerous. And," she continued, "advise the airport manager to discreetly clear the area of personnel."

Janna was repeatedly punching Ian's cell number into her own as she gave her instructions, cursing the automatic voice messaging she was being redirected to. Just then, the lone female clerk in the room looked up from her own telephone. She'd been in the midst of taking a message for Officer Logan from Lou Howard. He'd located Albert Cowan's missing boat at Gravenhurst Wharf, tied to a floating dock in the construction area. There was a single diver's air tank in it, she said, and traces of blood spatter on the deck and side. Sergeant Howard required an officer to secure the area and a technician with a blood Indent-a-Kit as soon as possible.

"He's still on the line," she nonchalantly advised Janna. "Do you want to speak with him while I contact the detachment office with his instructions?"

"Lou!" Janna practically shouted. "Drop what you're doing and get over to Taboo immediately. I'll fill you in when I meet you there, but Ian could be in danger. I'll need a Kevlar vest, radio and two more officers to go with me to the hotel."

"Wait a minute," Lou cautioned. "Just how many bodies do you think I have available? I've only got one more man locally, and he can't be here for ten minutes. He's actually on his way in from Doe Lake and that's closer to the airport. It'll be better if I turn him around and send him back there, but that's it for manpower."

"What about this guy here? Can he come with me?"

"Babcock's orders are to remain at the station until relieved, Janna. He's already on restricted duty from an earlier injury. No way I'm going to let him—"

"Okay, okay," Janna interrupted. "I've got to move, Lou. Now."

"Well then, have Babcock call Matt Finnerty at Orillia Headquarters and tell him you've posted one officer at the airport and that he needs backup. You and I can go to Taboo to find Ian."

"Murdoch and Mrs. de Sa are in danger. Have you got that?" Janna said as she ran to her car, strapping on a vest that Babcock had thrust at her on the way out the door. It took longer to get through the security gate at Taboo than it did to actually drive there, especially at the speeds she had managed.

27

EVEN THOUGH THE KNOCK startled Steve Roman, his gun hand never wavered. Murdoch turned his head slightly toward the door, catching Xiomara's eye long enough to see her shake her head and nod to the bag on the bed. Ian got the message—if he opened that bag and there were no gold coins, the two of them would likely wind up dead. They would more than likely wind up dead anyway.

As the departing bellhop closed the door, with only a fraction of a second to act, Ian swung the remaining bag off the bed, aiming directly at the man holding the gun. Sidestepping, Roman took the hit on the left hip, rolled with the motion, and was only knocked slightly backward. He managed to retain his balance and, with Murdoch still following through, instinctively struck out. The metallic silencer of his gun came down against Ian's head, dropping him like a stone. Murdoch fell face forward on the floor, blood erupting from the point of impact behind his right ear.

With the toe of his shoe, Roman prodded the cop's shoulder. Nothing. A line of blood began to soak through his collar to stain the carpeting. He was still alive, but the American immediately appreciated the difference between hitting a cop and killing one. Even if he was later identified, chances of extradition from the States for simple assault were negligible. He snatched the bag up, leaving Murdoch where he lay. It was heavy, heavy enough for a shit-load of something, but he had to admit he had no idea how much gold coins should weigh.

Xiomara, momentarily rooted to the spot in shock, began to recover. As she moved to Ian, praying that he was still alive, Roman pushed her away.

"Don't even think about it," he growled. "You attract enough attention as it is. If you get blood on those pretty clothes you'll do nothing but raise suspicion. And believe me, if that happens you'll get the same treatment as your boyfriend."

For a moment, Roman stood quietly at the doorway listening. He peered through the peephole but it was too low and its view too distorted to be certain what was in the hallway. It looked like someone from housekeeping at an open doorway in the direction opposite the exit. He counted to ten, composing himself, while keeping a close eye on both Murdoch and the woman. Removing the silencer from the barrel of the automatic, he folded an empty suit bag over the gun before waving it toward a terrified Xiomara.

"Okay," he announced at last. "Out the door, lady. You and I are going for a little ride. Just walk nice and slow to the elevator and we'll get out of here without anyone else getting hurt."

There was no one else in the hallway except an attractive blonde woman wheeling a linen trolley. Roman leered at her, then steered Xiomara to the elevator. The two of them were silent during the short ride down to the lobby. Casually, with Xiomara leading, they crossed the reception area and walked to the parking lot. As Xiomara turned toward her own vehicle, Steve Roman, just another happy tourist at the end of a relaxing vacation, redirected her to a white half-ton truck thirty yards away. He waited while she got in the passenger side, threw Jose de Sa's bag in the rear cargo box, and slid into the driver's seat.

"I have a jet at the airport," he said, laying the suit bag and gun across his lap. "You act nice and cool and I might just let you live."

"You're a fool if you think you can get away with this," Xiomara blurted between sobs. "Don't you know who you're dealing with?"

"Oh honey, I know exactly who I'm dealing with." Roman actually laughed. "I've been a flunky for these bastards for years. There's enough money in that bag to keep me for a long time in Mexico. Now, stop blubbering and wipe the snot off. It's not very becoming of a lady."

Xiomara wiped her face as they carefully pulled away from the northern exit of the Taboo lot, left toward Bracebridge on the secondary route he'd mapped out as the least obvious. He intentionally kept well within the speed limit. Normally, this would have been one of the more scenic drives in Muskoka, but neither Roman nor Xiomara took time to admire the view.

28

LOGAN FLASHED HER BADGE to security and requested that he call the front desk. She needed a room number and directions for Mrs. Xiomara de Sa. By the time she wheeled into the circular drive at reception, a clerk was waiting with the required information, handing her a slip of paper and pointing out the directions. He advised Janna as she rushed by that Mrs. de Sa had called for a luggage pick up nearly ten minutes before.

Logan pushed the elevator button for the third floor. When it opened, a bellhop was standing there with a suitcase.

"Is that Mrs. de Sa's?" Janna asked, once again flashing her tin.

"Yeah, I'm taking it to her car." He showed Janna the keys. "It's a rental."

"How many people in the room?"

"Three. Two men and Mrs. de Sa."

"Can they see the car from the room?"

"I dunno. Maybe, I guess."

"Okay, listen carefully. I want you to lock the bag in the trunk, pocket the keys, then go straight to the front desk. Wait there till either Sergeant Howard or I come for you, and don't let anyone else have those keys."

Walking directly but casually to Room 326, Janna listened closely at the door. Only one muffled voice was audible, male and insistent with an American accent. At an open door three rooms along, a chambermaid appeared with her linens and cleaning cart. Janna forced her into the empty room, finger to her lips to warn against making noise.

Again, Janna showed her police badge, instructing the maid to immediately go to the front desk and stay there until further notice. Before the young Jamaican woman hurried off, Janna relieved her of her master pass card. She frantically searched the maid's trolley for something, anything, to hide the obvious bulk of her Kevlar vest and gun. The only thing large enough was an oversized white guest robe. Quickly she stuffed her radio in one large pocket, gun in the other.

In the hallway once more, she rolled the cart towards Room 326, just as the door opened and two people emerged. The woman, likely de Sa, was in front of a man carrying an empty suit bag over his arm. He smiled tightly at Janna as he closed the door, taking a moment to hang a Do Not Disturb notice on the handle. There was no sign of Murdoch and, Janna guessed, the stranger was probably shielding a weapon behind the bag. It was pressed tightly against Xiomara de Sa's back.

The elevator lobby was just out of sight of the room. Janna waited until she heard the elevator's arrival before using the pass card to open 326. On the floor, bleeding from a gash on the side of his head, lay Ian Murdoch.

"Officer down," Janna spoke into her radio, fighting to keep the anxiety from her voice. "Room 326, Taboo Resort. Urgent."

"What's your 20?" Lou Howard's voice responded. "I'm almost at the gate."

"I'm leaving the room now. In pursuit of a male suspect,

over six feet with fair hair, tan slacks and light blue golf shirt. Possible hostage situation."

She propped the door open with a chair and ran to the fire exit stairway. Reaching ground level, she burst through the emergency door into the parking lot, almost immediately spotting Xiomara de Sa's rental car exactly where the bellhop had said it would be. There was no one near it and no sign of either Steve Roman or his hostage. Just pulling away from the last spot before the automated exit, however, was a white pick-up truck. An elegant woman in the passenger seat turned dark, panic-stricken eyes toward Janna. The driver was Steve Roman. Roman, Agent Jacks had warned, was a dangerous man.

Running to her car she pressed the transmit button on her radio. "This is Logan, with a description of the vehicle en route to Muskoka Airport. Watch for a late-model white Ford pick-up with two occupants, male driving and female passenger, probable hostage, headed to your location. Approach with caution, armed and dangerous. Do not allow access to the Lear jet parked in your vicinity." Rapidly she repeated the message.

Lou Howard responded instantly.

"Coming through the gate at Taboo. Chopper already in the air out of Orillia with three Swat officers and Superintendent Finnerty. Eta at Muskoka Airport approximately twelve minutes."

As he crested the hill to the resort entrance, Lou Howard saw Janna's unmarked car leaving the opposite end of the property.

"Lou," his radio barked. "You look after Ian, he's in the room, unconscious and injured. Secure the room and stay with him until EMS arrives. Suspect is headed north on Road 17, so I'm going south to approach the airport via the Gravenhurst entrance."

"Copy, Logan. I'm 10-8, leaving my vehicle."

"Final instructions, Lou?"

"Just get the bastard."

29

JANNA LOGAN had the accelerator to the floor travelling up the eastern service road from Gravenhurst to the Muskoka Airport. She took a gamble that she could beat the pick-up on the slower back road west of Highway 11.

Sure enough, as she wheeled behind a small block building near the entry to the tarmac, there was no sign of either the truck or her suspect. Trying to recall the identifying numbers of the jet, she glanced over the handful of visible aircraft belonging to Muskoka's summer millionaires and movie stars. Skidding to a halt, she threw open the door and ran to the terminal building. Racing inside she immediately ran into an OPP officer concealed at the entrance to a small office. He looked at her in disbelief until she realized she was still wearing the hotel robe. The officer had his gun drawn, challenging her for identification.

"Shit," she shouted to him. "I'm Logan! That white half-ton will be here any second." As she struggled out of the robe he saw the Kevlar vest and lowered his weapon. "The chopper should be here any minute as well, with three Swat sharp shooters. The woman in the truck is a hostage and must be protected, and the guy's dangerous. He'll make an attempt to—"

She never finished the sentence. At that moment Roman's rented truck entered the parking lot from the northwest. Logan and the uniform watched helplessly as it sailed past, straight toward the waiting Lear.

"Christ," she swore in disgust. "The gate is wide open for him."

Driving onto the tarmac, the vehicle stopped near the entrance door of the aircraft. The big American emerging from the cab reached into the cargo box and easily lifted a suitcase onto the ground. Rapping on the side window of the vehicle, he motioned to Xiomara de Sa and began walking to the jet. The woman exited the truck and stood momentarily in front of it. Her head turned right and left as if she were looking for someone. Logan wondered if she was considering making a run for it. Even at that distance, however, Roman's weapon was obvious, tucked into the waistband beneath his shirt.

"Look, I'm in plain clothes and he shouldn't be able to recognize me," Janna said to the young officer. "I'm going to walk out of here and get in my car. If I can drive between him and the woman, I'll try to separate them and get her to safety. If not, I'll drive to the nose wheel of the aircraft to prevent his takeoff. He'll probably make an attempt to stop me, might even shoot or, most likely, grab the hostage to get me to move."

Roman had finished opening the cabin and loading his

bag. Unwilling to take his eyes from Xiomara, he'd simply tossed the suitcase inside and was turning back to the truck.

"Get as close as you can when he's distracted, but don't shoot under any circumstances. With both a jet full of fuel and the hostage between you, it's too risky. We need time for the Swat boys to get here." With that, Janna was out the door and into the parking area, walking casually toward her vehicle.

While still only halfway across the lot she heard the *whap-whap-whap* of the incoming chopper's rotor. Roman had fully opened the Lear's door and pulled down the steps. Janna could see his head snap upward as he recognized the sound. Over the oncoming roar of the engines she could see him take out his weapon and point at his hostage, waving for her to move toward the jet even as he ran to grab her. In the car and moving, Janna could tell she was too late to intercept him. Instead, she drove to block the front wheel.

At the last moment Roman saw her car up against the nose wheel. He fired two rapid shots. One bullet slammed through the radiator, into the engine block, and ricocheted away. The other smashed the rear side window. Janna fell across the front seat and opened the passenger side door, away from the line of fire, crawling out onto the asphalt. The chopper was immediately overhead, its downdraught billowing up clouds of dust. Roman knelt on the tarmac near the entry gangway, waving his gun, undecided whether his greatest threat came from the car or the helicopter.

"This is the police, Mr. Roman," Matt Finnerty boomed threateningly from a loudspeaker in the belly of the chopper. "Drop your weapon and let the woman go. You're surrounded and you have no escape."

The laser sights of the Swat Team's weapons trained on Roman, dotting the doorway and crisscrossing his face and chest. He knew he was dead if he made a move, but there was always a chance they wouldn't fire so close to a hostage.

"Don't be stupid," Finnerty continued. "It's over. Let the girl go."

The dust propelled by the helicopter rotors cleared. Roman stood, wiped grit from his stinging eyes, then dropped both arms to his side. The gun in his right hand, he slowly bent and placed it on the ground. He wondered how all this had happened so fast. He'd had it made in the shade, a million dollars in his hands, and suddenly it all went for shit. How in hell did they know who he was? That motherfucker Manuel Ortiz must have set him up.

While Logan and the uniformed officer kept Roman in their sights, the helicopter landed at the rear of the jet. Swat members were first out, automatic rifles at the ready. They surrounded Roman, shouting instructions and securing him face down on the hot tarmac. An officer quickly retrieved Roman's gun and handed it to the Superintendent as he emerged.

Janna, meanwhile, made a beeline for Xiomara. She led her, white faced and shaking violently, to sit on the truck running board, away from the action. Janna sat beside her, held her shoulder tight and comforted her.

"Your man in the States got your message, Mrs. de Sa. He put out an alert and found that, coincidentally, they'd been tracking Steve Roman since he left Florida. We think Roman killed Lintz when he realized you had the coins. We'll have to hold them, of course. The coins are evidence. Somewhere down the line they'll be returned if it's shown that you're the rightful owner."

Janna pointed to the suitcase lying at the top of the aircraft stair. "Are they in that bag? "

Xiomara simply turned to her, hazel eyes full of tears, and shook her head.

"Are they in the other bag, in the trunk of your car at the hotel?"

Again Xiomara shook her head. "I don't know where the coins are."

"Oh God." Janna walked to meet Matt Finnerty and passed along the bad news.

"No, it can't be. Ian wouldn't be that stupid." Finnerty plunged both hands into his jacket pockets. "There must be another answer."

He had double-checked Xiomara de Sa's alibi after reading that she'd been in the hotel the whole day her husband was killed. The desk clerk, however, reported that Mrs. de Sa had left at noon—with a man in an unmarked police car, he'd insisted. She hadn't returned until late that afternoon.

"Why would Ian lie?" he'd muttered out loud. It had been Ian, after all, who'd said she had an ironclad alibi covering the period up until the resort manager informed her that her husband had been in an accident.

Lost in thought, Finnerty became aware of an approaching siren's piercing wail. Matt turned toward Logan.

"Did someone call the paramedics?"

Janna didn't have an opportunity to answer before both an ambulance and police cruiser pulled up. Babcock smiled out from behind the wheel of the cruiser as Ian Murdoch pulled himself out of the passenger's seat.

"Did we miss all the fun?" Babcock asked.

Murdoch had a large, hastily applied bandage on his head. He was unsteady on his feet, but otherwise seemed as normal as Janna had ever seen him. He walked directly to Matt.

"What to hell went down, is Mrs. de Sa all right?" He demanded, unable to see Xiomara where she rested on the step of the truck.

"We've got Steve Roman in custody," Matt said. "He was attempting to escape with Mrs. de Sa when Officer Logan blocked his aircraft."

Ian didn't appear to be listening. He located Xiomara at the truck and rushed over. When she spotted him she sprang up. He held her tight, her brown hair falling around his face.

"Oh, for Christ sake, don't tell me they were in cahoots. Ian, you can't be that stupid." Finnerty was speaking to himself.

"No, he can't." Logan had quietly joined him. Together they stood, watching Murdoch and Xiomara de Sa.

With his arm around Xiomara's waist, Ian walked back to join the others.

"I think we should go to the hospital. She's in shock and the paramedics tell me I have to be checked for a concussion. If you people have it all wrapped up, I'll go with Mrs. de Sa in the ambulance."

Finnerty and Logan nodded their assent while attendants helped Xiomara to the waiting vehicle. As Ian was about to get in, Finnerty took his arm.

"We haven't found the coins." He looked to where Xiomara was waiting for Murdoch. "She says she doesn't know where they are."

Ian's eyes were glassy, barely holding it together.

"Maybe there never were any."

30

MATT FINNERTY had finished a two-martini lunch before returning to the office. He said a few Hail Mary's, praying his suspicions were wrong. Many a good man had been seduced by those two companions, however—gold and greed.

His Personal Assistant buzzed through. "J.T. Murdoch is on line three."

"I tried to get Ian all morning, Matt," J.T. began, "and I haven't been able to reach him. Sorry to bother you again, but you're the only one I know to pass along a message."

"I'll track him down J.T. What is it?"

"Well, when we were involved with young Crawford, selling those Miss Liberty coins, we put out a notice to all our Canadian dealers."

Matt sat straight up in his chair, instantly alert.

"We asked them to notify us if anyone was wanting to buy or sell this particular coin. Anyway, we got a call from a dealer in Barrie a little while ago. A man wants to sell twenty of them. Because he wants cash for the sale, the dealer asked him to return at three this afternoon. It takes him that long to collect thirty-seven thousand dollars in cash. I don't know if it's relevant, but I thought I'd pass it along."

"It certainly is, J.T.. What's the address for this dealer in Barrie?"

As he wrote down the information, Matt rubbed sweat from his forehead.

"Thanks a million. I owe you big time," Finnerty concluded, looking at his watch. It was two fifteen. He tore the address from the scratch pad and was about to hang up.

"Oh, by the way," J.T. squeezed in his big news. "Tell Ian that I have a clean bill of health. My cancer's in remission."

The Superintendent barely took time to congratulate the elder Murdoch before bounding out of the office, past a startled assistant, and down to the parking lot. He could make Barrie in twenty minutes easy. The coin shop was on the main street, downtown, but he knew the area well. He'd attended court just around the corner when he was the oldest rookie in the local detachment.

From his car, driving one-handed, he used his personal cell to call Bracebridge. Ian Murdoch and Xiomara de Sa, he was told, had both checked out of hospital that morning.

An eternity later, Matt confirmed that he was alone in the shop before asking a clerk for the manager. The coin dealer turned out to be small, bald and overly plump, the fold of his gut hanging over his belt. A coin merchant if Finnerty had ever seen one, all he needed was a black eyepiece to fit the stereotype. Fred Wilms didn't have time to be intimidated by the big Irish cop, and he certainly wasn't happy to hear he might lose the profits he'd calculated on resale of the coins. But it wouldn't do to piss off the cops. It was a lesson he'd learned early in his business.

Hasty arrangements were made in confidence with Wilms,

who left an attaché case of money with Matt Finnerty in his
back office. Finnerty contemplated pulling his gun, wondering if he should call for back up. No, he decided, he just
couldn't do that to a friend. He heard the electronic chime of
the front door, a short muffled conversation, and then foot-
steps. A moment later the office door opened, a man stepped
in and Wilms quickly departed.

"If you touch that money I'll have to arrest you. Please don't
make me do that."

Lou Howard, more ashamed than alarmed, meekly stepped
away from the desk empty-handed.

EPILOGUE

THEY DROVE TO GRAVENHURST IN SILENCE. Howard didn't have to tell his story. Matt had reviewed the log of all police boats on Lake Muskoka. Someone, whose signature was illegible, had taken one out two nights earlier. Illegible or not, the handwriting had been instantly recognizable to Finnerty. When he asked Howard where the remaining gold coins were, he could have guessed the answer to that, as well. Matt finally reached Ian on his cell phone at the Community Office in town, shooting the shit with Babcock. Finnerty told him to meet them at the Wharf.

"Have Babcock make a police boat available. But," Finnerty was emphatic, "don't let the kid come along."

At the Wharf, with an oversized OPP ball cap covering his newest bandage, Ian watched two men walking toward him. They were probably his two closest and oldest friends. Both looked pale and nervous, neither offering a greeting as they joined him on the boat. They headed out into the lake.

"Where to?" Ian asked.

"Your place, of course." It was the most that the normally talkative Finnerty would say for the next half-hour.

Curiosity aside, the run to Ian's island was made in dead silence. Murdoch pieced much of the jigsaw together in his mind. He knew Orby Lintz never had the coins, and that Xiomara didn't have them, either. Steve Roman didn't have them, or he wouldn't have put the dent in Murdoch's head while looking for them. And, sure as shit, Matt Finnerty didn't have them. For all his skill and bravado, the boss was scared to death of water. Lou Howard, however, was the final, elusive piece. The only unknown was how Matt, that big, dumb, lovable leprechaun, had figured it all out.

Lou led the way from Ian's dock, past the rocky head of land to a small outbuilding. Once there, he crawled under the tool shack and retrieved a grubby pillowcase. Holding it out to Finnerty, Lou winced at the sound of jingling coins. Ian nodded to the cottage and the three friends retraced their steps, waiting while Murdoch unlocked the door.

They spread the coins on the kitchen table, staring in disbelief for several minutes. A thought pounded through Murdoch's brain: four dead, a long-serving police officer's career in ruins, and friendships destroyed. It was the curse of gold, the price of greed.

Matt Finnerty sat opposite his two junior officers. From beneath tired, hooded eyes he said, "This is how you're going to write your report, Lou."

His soft Irish voice was almost a whisper. "On the advice of Inspector Ian Murdoch you went to the crash site at Twin Rocks in search of evidence. When you sighted the tackle box in shallow water, you secured it and immediately called for further instructions. Unfortunately, you weren't able to reach him so you came to the island. Murdoch wasn't here, of course."

Murdoch and Howard stared at Finnerty. Was this for real?

"In the interim, you decided to return the weighted box to the lake, where you'd mount surveillance. The intention was to identify Peter Crawford's murderer, suspected to be Orby Lintz, while collecting sufficient evidence to arrest him for the murders of both Crawford and his mother."

Lou Howard shook his head.

"It won't work, Matt."

"Shut up and listen. The speed of events prevented either of you from placing the evidence in lock up. You called me because you thought it prudent to place the coins with a senior officer from headquarters."

"And the coin dealer in Barrie?"

"We needed to authenticate the coins and get an assessment of their value," Finnerty explained. When his companions finally nodded their assent he continued. "Lou, I want your request for early retirement on my desk tomorrow morning. I'll see you get every benefit available for your years of loyal service. I'm sure a doctor will corroborate the levels of stress you've been working under, considering you've recently lost a valuable friend and fellow officer."

A horrific vision of Jean Musgrave flashed before Ian's eyes. It had never occurred to him that his struggle with Frank Airscliff, and the stray shot that had left Jean lying in a pool of blood, could have affected Lou as much as it had him. Lou had been the rock, the guy who stuck his neck out and cleaned up the mess of a vile investigation. Lou had been pure gold.

The disappointment was evident in Finnerty's voice, however. "Service and loyalty aside, I have to tell you I'm saddened that a man of your integrity and devotion could be corrupted. You have to understand there's no place left for you on the job."

Ian started to speak but Matt was unwilling to allow any question or variation from his plan.

"You'll write your report to agree with Howard's. Make a few minor discrepancies so that it won't look contrived, but have both reports on my desk tomorrow. Most importantly, Janna Logan should never hear about any of this. Okay now, let's get back to the Wharf. First, however, I want to speak with you alone, Ian."

Lou, clearly relieved, stood and made his way to the door. As he pushed the screen open he turned to his friends. Finnerty seemed to read his mind.

"We'll never speak of this again, is that clear?"

When Howard was out of earshot, Ian had difficulty keeping the emotion from his voice. "Thanks, Matt. It may not be right, but it's the decent thing to do."

"Don't thank me, you've got a lot of work to do. I want you to stay close to Howard. I'm afraid he may attempt something even more stupid."

They exchanged a long look.

Matt changed the subject. "A pilot from the charter service is coming from Florida to take their jet back. He'll take Mrs. de Sa with him at the same time. You know, Ian, she's going to be a very wealthy widow. Are you even the slightest bit interested? She certainly looks like she's interested you."

"Thanks, but no thanks. I can't stand the heat, let alone the humility. Besides, I drove Xiomara back to the hotel to get her bags and we had a long talk. I'm not ready for a relationship. Not now, maybe never."

Gathering up the pillowcase of gold coins, they began making their own way to the dock. They saw a listless Lou Howard waiting, seemingly incapable of deciding whether to just stare at the lake or actually get in the boat.

"What about Steve Roman?" Ian asked. "What's become of him?"

"Singing like a bird. Hoping to cop a plea, no doubt. No way he wants to go back to the States as long as Manuel Ortiz and his friends are free. Roman's testimony could supply the evidence to finally lock them up if he gets his deal to stay here. Just think, Ian, small-town cops lit a match that could burn down a multi-national money-laundering operation. God knows what other crooked games these bastards were involved in."

For a moment, Finnerty's mood seemed to lighten. He looked first to Ian, then into the distance at Lou who had finally chosen to sit in the boat, with proud affection.

"Let's get back to the Wharf before this damn stuff corrupts me," Matt smiled.

While Ian was untying the boat, Lou confided in him.

"I can't explain what came over me. When I figured out the gold must be near Twin Rocks I went out on my own. It was just curiosity at first, but when I dove down and brought them up so easily, something just took over. Then I saw the coins and held them in my hand. I don't know how I ever figured I'd get away with it. And me a cop. Just how stupid can one man get?"

"Don't bother, Lou. I don't need an explanation."

"To tell you the truth, I've wanted out of the force for some time. My wife's been a nervous wreck ever since you were shot and, well, after Jean. God, Ian, I'm sorry I let everyone down."

The boat rocked in the water as Finnerty stepped in.

"If you don't mind, Matt," Murdoch said. "I'd like to stay here a while. I'll call Albert to pick me up later. Hey, Lou, let's you and I have dinner tonight. Pick you and the wife up at your place around six, okay? I'll expense the whole thing, and Finnerty can pick up the tab."

The big Irishman nodded. "Last time, though."

Ian watched the boat ride out the long waves, pushed by a north wind until it disappeared around the lighthouse at the Narrows. The afternoon sun had turned the cottage into an oven. He took a minute to open the windows, waiting outside while the breeze had a chance to cool it off. The plastic deck chair was hot so he eased himself down, reclined, and closed his eyes.

He was startled by three blasts of the RMS *Segwun*'s steam whistle as the vessel slipped close by his island. Out of habit, he waved at the passengers. Over the public address system he heard an unwelcome announcement. "And that's Sea Gull Island, folks. Where a famous OPP detective lives."

Ian made another mental note to put a stop to that notoriety. He was just a cop, even if it was an ambition that had consumed him since high school. His only desire was to be the best he was capable of. Since Caitlin died, ambition had been farthest from his mind. And then came Xiomara. He could have a comfortable life with her. Better yet, it would be in Florida, a long way from the nightmares that plagued his sleep. Eventually, perhaps, he could learn to love her. But it wasn't to be.

A kept man? Never. He shook his head. Was it Caitlin? It didn't matter, anyway.

There were no boats in sight so he stripped down and dove from his dock into Lake Muskoka. The cool water was invigorating, cleansing. His mind clear, he hauled himself out and went to dress. The late August sun was lowering on the horizon. It was time. Ian punched out the number for Cowan's Marina.

The youngest of eight children, Liam Dwyer was born in Eganville, Ontario, in 1923. He received his primary and secondary education in Cobalt and Kirkland Lake. Joining the Canadian Navy in 1942, he served as a Petty Officer on the HMCS *Sarnia*, which was assigned to convoy duty in the North Atlantic and to mine sweeping off Newfoundland and Nova Scotia.

After the war, he worked for A.V. Roe (later called Hawker Siddley) on the Orenda and Iroquois gas turbines, the latter being used as the power plant for the Avro Arrow. He retired from the company after thirty-seven years in senior management positions.

With Mary, his wife of sixty-two years, Liam enjoys their home on Lake Muskoka at Gravenhurst and vacationing in Deerfield Beach, Florida. They have three sons, Liam James of Bracebridge, Gregory John of Regina, and Joseph Timothy of Fort Lauderdale.

Liam's first Inspector Murdoch mystery novel, *Murder in Muskoka*, was published in 2004.

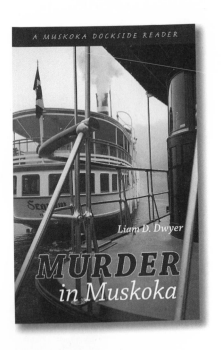

Murder in Muskoka, the debut Ian Murdoch mystery, begins with Ian resting at his island cottage on Lake Muskoka, trying to recover from the death of his wife. When a body floats ashore, he's immediately thrust back into his role as a homicide investigator for the Ontario Provincial Police. Things get even more complicated with the discovery of a headless skeleton on an abandoned farm in nearby Vankoughnet.

Along with the young female officer assigned to help him, Murdoch is rapidly drawn into a web of intrigue and treachery that involves the history of World War II German prisoners at Camp 20 in Gravenhurst, the oldest operating steamboat on the continent, and an elderly lady with an astounding secret she's kept for nearly sixty years.

Available through your bookseller / ISBN 0-9736208-0-3